I0638619

Rejuvenation

A Novel
of the Near Future

Patrick Fanning

ArtWorks Press
Graton, California

ArtWorks Press
9155 Grey Street
Graton, CA 95444
www.fanningartworks.com

MANUFACTURED IN THE UNITED STATES OF AMERICA

LIBRARY OF CONGRESS
CATALOGING-IN-PUBLICATION DATA
FANNING, PATRICK
REJUVENATION: A NOVEL OF THE NEAR FUTURE
ISBN 978-0-692-02805-6

Down, down, down into the darkness of the grave
Gently they go, the beautiful, the tender, the kind;
Quietly they go, the intelligent, the witty, the brave.
I know. But I do not approve. And I am not resigned.

- Edna St. Vincent Millay

Contents

1. In the Orrery

On the morning his life started to fall apart, Dr. Ben Rasmussen was a little late getting to work. He slipped into his office at Kalimer Pharmaceuticals and set down his steaming cup of chox, wincing to see a v-mail from Dr. Trujib Kapoor already waiting for him.

It was a short clip, Dr. Kapoor looking sideways and scornfully out of the screen, saying in his too-quiet voice, "Dr. Rasmussen, would you please join me in my office at thirteen o'clock this afternoon? I'd like a word with you."

As a member of the executive caste, Kapoor scorned using any kind of avatar for his v-mail, appearing unaltered with his shining bald dome and large pores. You'd think the old man would at least use a grooming filter.

The image froze at the end of this curt message. Ben sipped carefully at his cup and stared at his handheld, as if the intensity of his gaze could force the Indian's bland features to yield more information. He looked at the header. The CC box was blank, indicating no copies to anyone and implying that this would be a private meeting.

Something was up. Something was not right. Kapoor was two levels above Ben, his boss's boss. It was a major breach of protocol for Kapoor to approach Ben directly. In twenty-three years with the firm, Ben had seldom met privately with anyone of the executive caste. It would have been more proper for Kapoor to pass his invitation through Ben's immediate supervisor, Cynthia Lim, and include her in the meeting. That way the daisy chain of command would be preserved. Executive, administrative, and technical levels would all be present and accounted for, everybody taking notes and covering ass.

Ben's favorite image of corporate life was a brass orrery he saw once in a science museum. It was a clockwork model of the solar system, designed to reproduce and predict the movement of the moon and planets. It was constructed when the earth was considered the center of the universe, and when celestial bodies were thought to move only in perfect Ptolemaic circles. So the earth was at the center and the sun and planets revolved around the earth, on complex cycles and epicycles of perfect circles. Like Kalimer Pharmaceuticals, the orrery was an insanely complex machine, designed on faulty principles, accomplishing everyday tasks in the most roundabout way possible, never really working the way you wanted it to.

Lately he had been feeling like smashing the orrery. It constrained him to following the same orbit day after day. It kept him from deviating from his proper round as a tiny brass moon of a tiny brass planet, kept him from finding out what was going wrong with his research. Whenever he asked the wrong question or suggested a change in procedure he was perceived as trying to move in an illegal ellipse, stripping the gears of the corporate orrery. Maybe some of his queries had got back to Kapoor, drawing his attention. To mix the metaphor, Kapoor hated to see a nail sticking up in his section of the corporate deck, although he usually delegated the pounding flat to others and didn't wield the hammer himself.

Ben considered asking his boss Cynthia about this, but hesitated. He was sure she was sleeping with Kapoor. She spent too much time in Kapoor's office. The two of them tended to arrive at the same time each morning. Cynthia seemed to have too easy a time getting her projects approved, her budgets okayed, her travel paid for. She had once or twice referred to her boss as "Trujib" rather than by his last name or his nickname, "Trudge." She was Chinese /Administrative and Trujib was Indian/Executive, so it would be a strained, unequal match, but maybe their common Asiatic ancestry drew them together. In his career, Ben had seen the Asians who dominated corporate life evolve from parasites surviving by imitating their hosts into the dominant species, their chief characteristic a caricature of oriental inscrutability. It was hard to discern any true substance behind the style.

Just then Cynthia called him.

"Ben, the weeklies are in from Durance. We should go over them."

"Okay, I'll grab them and join you in a few minutes."

He scrolled back on his handheld and found the report from Durance Corporation. Scanning it on the way to Cynthia's office, his hopes fell. The 516 prisoners in the RC12 study, mostly 'Spanic and AA non-violents, were still not doing so well. Actually, there were only 510 subjects now. Another six had dropped out of the study: one paroled, one transferred to another facility, two brought up on charges, three "disqualified for cause," whatever that meant. For the remaining 510, gains in physical strength, cognitive functioning, and immune response were still modest--nowhere near the results he had produced with rats and monkeys. And the side effects were more severe: migraine headaches, agitation, even a few petit mal seizures.

It was frustrating. Composite lifespan predictors for the men and women on RC12 were only 4.3 years longer than the control group--statistically significant, but hardly exciting in view of the side effects. He shook his head, mystified. Why was a regimen that nearly doubled the lifespan of animals just not working on humans?

He went to the men's room to tidy up. In the mirror his fifty-nine-year-old face looked splotched, puffy, and saggy. He flexed his sore knees and craned his stiff neck. He compared the shape of his right thumb to his left. It was definitely swollen at the base where it had been bothering him.

Futurists liked to say that his generation was the first with a real chance at immortality, or at least significant longevity in the 200 to 300 year range. The way he felt today, he and

11

his colleagues had better hurry. He'd be sixty next month. His mind slipped into a familiar groove, one it had been gouging out of the gray matter every birthday since he was thirty-five: Am I halfway yet? If I live to be 100, I still have forty percent of my life ahead of me. If I can stretch it to 120, I'm only half way to death. 200? 250? On that scale I'm still an adolescent. I still have lots of time. Don't I?

There was a spot of chox on the off-white overvest that identified him as a research scientist, part of the technical caste. He dabbed at it with a wet paper towel. Considering how long it had been since he had done any real lab work, he should really be wearing the gray of the administrative class, a promotion he both yearned for and dreaded. At this rate, he'd probably never wear the gold of the executive level. His wife Louise had bought him an expensive gold vest for his birthday last year, and it was still hanging in his closet, unworn. What good would it do him to live another 200 years, if he was stuck living days like today, over and over?

Ben longed for the glory days of his youth. Thirty years ago, when he was still in grad school on a Kalimer fellowship, he had spliced what came to be known as the Judas Kiss virus. He still liked to think of it privately as the Rasmussen Marker Virus. His marker virus would only infest abnormal, damaged, or pre-cancerous cells, tagging them for removal by artificial macrophages developed by other young hotshots of the day. The Judas Kiss was a key component of Kalimer's first true cancer prevention drug. Back then, it was the "Soaring Twenties," a time of discovery and expansion, when anything seemed possible. Ben was sure he would quickly earn down his student loans and entrepreneurial grants-in-aid and shoot to the top of Kalimer's fully vested executive caste. From that lofty vantage he would help bring a longer and happier life to all. He himself would have it all: long life, riches, the satisfaction of a career spent helping others, making a difference for the whole human race.

He splashed water on his face and rubbed hard, trying to wake himself up, wishing he could restore by external friction the internal spark of creativity he used to have. Getting older was a special torture for genetic chemists. Like the nuclear physicists of yore, they tended to peak early. He knew that his best days were long behind him. If he hadn't made his mark by now, he never would. That's why he was setting so much store by RC12. It contained several components designed to make the rejuvenated patient not just live longer but feel younger, act younger, and hopefully think younger.

Ben trudged up the stairs to the next floor instead of taking the elevator. Perhaps the exertion would pump a little extra blood to his tired brain. He'd need all the smarts he could muster. His right hip hurt. He already had implants of stem-cell cartilage in his hips and knees and one ankle. It was about time to renew the right hip.

2. Cohorts

He knocked lightly on the door marked Cynthia Lim and his boss called out "Enter" from within. Cynthia was New Hong Kong Chinese, petite and proper behind her desk, in a slate gray linen overvest, with matte black hair in a conservative spike. Ben's eyes swept Cynthia's window with its thirtieth floor view of the Santa Rosa waterfront and the haze of San Francisco Bay beyond. Ben hadn't had a window office himself for many years.

He asked, "What do you know about Dr. Kapoor wanting to see me at thirteen?" He tried to keep his voice light and casual.

Cynthia's features froze several degrees below her usual cool, then her eyes rolled up and to the left, as if to consult vast cognitive data banks. She tilted her head, shrugged, and opened her empty palms in innocent denial. Search over, nothing retrieved.

"No clue," she said. "News to me."

"What should I do?"

The tilt, shrug, empty palms again. "See what he wants," she said.

Ben nodded and decided to change the subject. Lim knew something but she wasn't talking. She should have been suspicious and curious, not calm and matter-of-fact. He pulled out his handheld. "Anyway, you wanted to go over the weeklies from Durance?"

"Right. But first, I have a surprise." She picked up a prescription pill bottle from her desk and handed it to him. He read the label.

"Rejuven?" he said, "that's what they're calling it? Rejuven?"

"Yes, Rejuven. Has a nice ring to it, doesn't it?"

"You don't think it's... I don't know, kind of obvious?"

"Not at all. It's been focus grouped and this is the one they preferred above all the other names."

Ben rotated the bottle and read out loud: "Take one capsule daily, for reversal of age symptoms?"

"That's right. Timed release formula for the mood elevators and hormone boosters."

"What about the cell clock stopper, and all the viral vectors? We've been injecting them separately."

"Marketing really wanted a single capsule, and the simulations say it will work."

"Maybe." He opened the bottle and shook out a handful of orange and white capsules. "These real?"

"Yes. Limited first run of 30,000 units, but the powers that be are getting excited. They're going to start showing them on InMates next week. No more injections, and they'll start calling it 'Rejuven,' not just 'the treatment.'"

"You know, Cynthia, as principle investigator I've always had serious reservations about that show. About advanced product placement in general."

"Oh Ben, I'd hardly call you principle investigator. You're on the team, but it is a team, you know. We all have our contributions to make. And we've been over the whole InMates thing before."

Ben nodded. It was a touchy subject and a battle he'd lost. InMates was a reality TV show on one of the high-number channels. In cheesy holographic 3D, InMates featured the romantic entanglements of real gay and lesbian couples in a men's low-security facility in Nebraska and a women's prison in Utah. Last season, Kalimer bought serious product placement, making their life-extension human trial a key plot point of the show. Several of the cast members were entered into the human trials of RC12, called simply "the treatment" on the show. The characters, helped by diet, exercise, and makeup as much as the drug, got younger and sexier, causing plot complications in the form of jealousy, breakups, screaming matches, and fistfights. It was all about building advance consumer interest in the RC12 treatment, which they were going to start calling "Rejuven," apparently.

Ben hated the whole idea. It was premature and misleading. At best it trivialized science and at worst corrupted scientific method. He considered most reality TV to be consumer porn, and in a meeting last year he had made the mistake of referring to televised drug trials as "pharma-tainment." He really should learn to keep his mouth shut, but some things just needed to be said.

He put the bottle back on Cynthia's desk. "I notice there's nothing about side effects."

She laughed. "We'll stick those in the pamphlet, small print."

"We've got serious problems with side effects in the trials." He turned his handheld toward her. "Mood swings, aggression, a couple of seizures."

"They're convicts, Ben. Not the most stable population

in the first place."

"And what about the dropout rate? Six more pulled from the study last week alone."

"Prison policy. They get transferred to another facility, get early release, have accidents—it's not something we can control."

"I thought Kalimer owned stock in Durance Corp. Doesn't that give us control?"

"Not as much as you'd think."

"It really messes up the data."

"I know, but they're doing the best they can."

Ben wondered if she was lying, or just incompetent. If she weren't sleeping with Kapoor, she wouldn't be human trials supervisor. She didn't really have the science background. More of a marketeer.

"Okay," he said, "But we've really got to find a way of tracking these people longer, over time. RC12..."

"Rejuven," she interrupted.

"Rejuven. You sure that's the best name? Rejuven implies you're going to get younger, but that's not what the drug does. We don't actually make you younger except on the cellular level: reset the telomere clock so that cells will divide accurately for maybe 130 years instead of ninety. And that's only if you start taking it young enough. If you're already ninety, you're out of luck."

"Nonagenarians are not our market anyway. They're way past their peak spending years. We want the thirty-five to forty-five cohort."

"Yeah, I realize they're the ones with the money." Ben said. Nonagenarians? Cohort? She was sounding like her paramour, Trujib Kapoor. "Ideally, we'd start people around age sixteen or eighteen, right after puberty."

"Why not at birth? Then we'd have customers for life."

"That would be a hormonal train wreck. RC12 induces a kind of artificial puberty. You don't want or need that until after real puberty."

"I was actually joking about the infants."

"I know. But I'm not. Rejuven, if that's really what I must call it, has some behavioral consequences that I'm just beginning to understand—changes in diurnal cycles, libido, reactivity. I don't see how we can even draft a complete list of the side effects. The data has too many holes in it."

"I'm starting a new group of white collar women offenders next week. That'll help."

"Not for long term sequelae. I'm still thinking I need to get onsite at some of these places, see what's going on, talk to the clinical techs and the subjects themselves."

"Oh, you wouldn't want to do that. There's so much red tape, and we have a protocol in place that keeps researchers and subjects apart. You know that."

"I don't see how I could bias data any worse than it's already screwed up. You know, in the old days, the scientists ran their own clinical trials, with help from grad students. It was all part of the university system, and the goal was furthering knowledge, not profit."

"And it was riddled with waste and political maneuvering."

Ben smiled. "You think we don't have waste and politics now?"

"At least it's minimized by focus on the bottom line."

"Right, that's what we say." Ben put the bottle back on her desk. "All I'm asking for is a quick trip around the Midwest, hit the units where we have the longest running trials, get in and out. I'll stay away from your precious InMates facilities in Omaha and Salt Lake—you'll never see me on camera."

"Interesting idea, Ben. I'll think about it."

Ben forced himself to smile and nod. He left her office, closing the door softly but feeling like slamming it. In Kalimer-speak, "Interesting idea" was code for "Not a chance in hell." And "I'll think about it" meant "I hate it."

3. Gateway Drug

Ben went straight to his desk and logged onto his Human Resources account. It was something he'd been doing more frequently in the last few months, at least once a week. Like scratching a chronic itch, he once more contemplated quitting Kalimer and going to work for some other outfit, one that would take his ideas more seriously, one that was more about R&D and less about show business and owning a piece of every kind of action there was. If any firms like that still existed.

The damn H. R. interface had been reconfigured again. He couldn't find his vesting history, or even a loan summary figure. Irritated, he folded up his handheld and stormed off to the elevators.

On seven, he walked into the fourth cube from the end and plunked down in the narrow plastic chair. They didn't want you hanging around H.R. too long, so the furniture was the most uncomfortable they could find.

Sally looked up from her screen.

"Hi Dr. Rasmussen. How are you today?" She pushed her glasses up and parked them in her blond hair. She was wearing bright yellow plastic earrings that matched her yellow clerical overvest.

"I'm fine, thanks," Ben said automatically. "How are you and Benji doing?"

"We're okay. His cold is better, but he's still coughing. What can I do for you?"

"I don't get this new interface," he said, showing her his handheld. "Why do they keep changing it? Doesn't it make more work for everybody in the long run?"

"It's all the mergers, ChemGen and the rest. Every time we acquire a new asset, the software has to be tweaked to shuffle the businesses together. Our interface is just the tip of a giant iceberg."

"It's more like a mudberg. I can't make any sense out of this." He passed her his handheld.

"Well, let's see," she said, scooting her chair next to him and pulling her glasses down. They had thick temple pieces, probably full of audio and emo link hardware. "This is your current master balance." Pointing to a figure that was distressingly large and in the negative column.

"That much?" Ben said. "Are you sure that's right?"

"Absolutely. We might change how we show it, but the computation is rock solid. That's where you stand."

"Show me how the computation works, again. If you don't mind."

She sighed, ever so slightly. "That part hasn't changed since we went over it last month. Here are your credits on the plus side: your Kalimer stock, your subsidiary holdings, your retirement account, your patent shares, your performance bonuses."

"And that adds up to this number here?" Ben pointed to a figure on the screen.

"That's right. And here are the debits, going back to your student loans and grants in aid at Stanford, your dissertation stipend, the first and second mortgages on your house and planes, a couple of re-fis, your current salary draw, benefit package. Kalimer has a lot invested in you—your education, your career, your current lifestyle. It all adds up to this figure."

Ben looked at the sum of what he owed to the company. "And the difference?"

"That's this number. Not quite vested yet."

That was an understatement. If Ben quit today, all his in-house corporate debt would come due. He'd owe Kalimer an amount that was over three year's salary, with no income or savigns to pay it. As a terminee, his inhouse debt would be outsourced to some predatory collection agency. He'd be bankrupt, unless he had another firm with deep pockets willing to pick up his tab. That wasn't likely, considering his age, level, and track record.

"So looking forward," he said, "How long till I'm vested?"

"Well, assuming nothing changes, it looks like... about eleven years to breakeven."

Breakeven. "Retiring" at age seventy-something, with nothing more than Social Security, that venerable pittance. RC12—no, Rejuven—would have to be a big success. It would have to make it to market, and his performance bonus would have to be sizable. It was his only way out.

"Thank you, Sally," he said, rising to leave. He smiled at her to show he didn't take the bad news personally. "I really appreciate you explaining all this. It's amazing how you stay on top of all the changes."

She smiled back. "Don't forget your 'vice.'" She passed him the handheld.

Ben drifted back to the elevators and stood slouched against the wall. He stared at the elevator lights. All six cars were moving away from him. He should have taken the stairs, if only for the exercise. He should hit the gym today.

He tried to console himself by thinking about people in Sally's position. She and her sickly toddler Benji lived with her mother in a tiny apartment. At her level, she'd probably never get vested. The sinking boat of her career was no more seaworthy than his. If only he had refused Kalimer's student loans, resisted that financial gateway drug, and somehow financed his education another way. He would have been free to hook up with a small startup after school. Maybe even start his own company, something that would be pure and lean and smart from top to bottom, something he could be proud of. Like his friend and roommate Pateesh, who did his graduate work in nano polymerization and parlayed six optical coatings patents into his own firm. Pateesh and Siri had asked Ben to join them after graduation, but he was already in too deep with Kalimer by then. And too fearful. In those days he wanted the security of a big company, whose investments in his tuition and board would guarantee him a job. Maybe if Rejuven didn't pan out, Pateesh would let him come work for them, buy out his debt for old time's sake and let him run a lab somewhere. No, not likely. He hadn't called or v-mailed his old friend in years.

The prospect of getting back to work was too daunting. When the elevator finally came, Ben pressed the button for nine, the gym floor. On the way up, his handheld rang. It was his wife Louise. He let it go to voicemail. Another thing he would do differently was not marry Louise right out of school. Play the field more, find someone more compatible, less cool, less focused on her own thing and more into him. She was such a hotshot in her field, it made Ben look bad.

4. Call It a Leg Day

In the gym Ben tried to remember if this was a core day, an arm day, or a leg day. Yesterday blended in to the day before and the day before that. His short-term memory for casual details was shit. Yet another symptom of the aging body. The worst one: the aging brain. Around age forty-five or fifty, more brain cells died than were replaced. Production of neurotransmitters declined and without those lovely happy juices like serotonin and its cousins, fewer of the remaining brain cells deigned to fire off in their accustomed pathways, shredding and clouding memory. In the worst case, plaques and tangles of the dreaded Alzheimer's syndrome formed and began the exquisite process of turning your brain into lumpy tapioca pudding.

That's what happened to Ben's mom, Alzheimer's. One day he came home from high school and she told him to put some bread in the candle instead of in the toaster. Nine months later she could not reliably remember his name, retreating into an embarrassed vagueness, then irritability, then outright aggression. Her irrational rages at her buttons and the chirping mocking birds in the magnolia tree finally forced Ben's dad to put her away. On all his visits home from college he would visit her in the "difficult ward," where she sat in a wheelchair cursing out the staff, her arms on short scarf tethers so she couldn't snatch other's belongings or scratch anyone easily. She was dead before he finished his undergraduate degree, and his dad was dead before he finished grad school. His dad died of a heart attack at age sixty. Ben always thought of his Dad's heart attack as a literally broken heart.

Call it a leg day. He sat down in the oblique hip machine and set the weights at seven. There was a time not so many years ago when he did this machine at eleven. But he was doing lighter weights and more reps these days, putting less strain on his arthritic joints, less pressure to squeeze and erode his thinning cartilage in knees and hips, shoulders and elbows. Two sets of fifteen, then on to the hip extension, two sets of fifteen, then the same on the leg curl machine. Reaching for a five-kilo weight with his right hand, his left hand came underneath it automatically to share the weight. He'd been doing that routinely for the last year or so. The joint at the base of his right thumb was perpetually sore. The cartilage was gone and it was bone on bone in two places. When he gripped too tightly, the pain flared like a discordant note in his ongoing mental soundtrack. So he used two hands often where a younger man would use one. And overall the soundtrack sucked. He really should get the joint replaced, but tapping the company health plan would put him another six months away from becoming vested.

Usually the familiar routine calmed him, improved his mood and mental focus. But not today. Today, he just felt old, tired, and on the downhill slope in so many ways: nearly sixty, arthritic, past his best years as a scientist, just going through the motions of his life. Just waiting to die, really. It was a vicious circle. The increasing aches and pains of getting older made you less active, more depressed. Your deteriorating mood made you even less active, less engaged in life, more focused on the aches and pains.

Ten years ago when he began working on RC1, the first version of what they were now calling Rejuven, Ben's key insight was to realize that feeling old and being old are too different things. He was reading a Kurt Vonnegut novel, where Eliot Rosewater advises washing an aspirin down with a glass of wine to cure the blahs. It made sense that if you can reduce pain and improve mood, you'll feel younger, and that's half the battle. His then fifty-year-old body was capable of doing many "young" things, but he didn't have the interest or energy to do them any more. If he could improve his mood and decrease pain symptoms in his knees, he'd be more likely to go jogging or for a walk or to a party—more likely to act young and feel young, regardless of his old body parts. The cool thing about being young is feeling young. Biochemically it's a matter of stimulants and hormones: energy both physical and sexual. Caffeine and testosterone will do it for a man, in the sort term, until the inevitable crash from the caffeine and plateau for the sex hormone. Rejuven took a more systemic approach, targeting the genes that produce proteins that stimulate the production of endorphins and natural hormones.

Ben passed up the leg extension machine. It put too much stress on his knees. He reclined on the squat machine, where he'd do some extra reps to make up for not doing the leg extensions. He pushed against the footplate, and the sled he was lying on moved back and upwards as his legs straightened. Each time he bent his knees and squatted down, he could turn his head slightly to the left and see into the next room, where Lila from the lab was running flat out on a treadmill.

She was long and lean, hardly an ounce of fat, pounding away like a machine. Her skin was tan and taut, her breasts like two lemons held tight in an elastic sports bra, her chiseled abs glistening with sweat, her bare arms and legs pumping like pistons.

Ben lost count of his repetitions on his machine, rested at full extension, and succumbed to a familiar fantasy. He was a shape shifter. No, more like a body jumper, a kind of vampire or alien who could take over other people's bodies, swap with them and become them, his mind/soul/personality suddenly in charge of a young, strong, capable body. Man or woman, it didn't matter. The thrill was the notion of being suddenly young again, the clock reset, but with all his own experience and memories intact. Young, but smart and mature, not young and dumb and naive.

It was one of his favorite pastimes, imaging how it would be. He'd see a fit young guy running along the bike path, and just swap places and be running along, suddenly twenty-three again, strong and pain free, with tons of tight cartilage in his knees, all the wind he wanted, cranking out eight minute mile after eight minute mile. Too bad about the personality of the young man, suddenly sixty years old in a painful body, looking out from dim eyes, sitting slumped on a bench, watching his former body jog away. Don't think about him. Think about what it would be like to jog into the woods, and take out the young man's wallet, and try to figure out who he is, who my new identity is, where he parked his car, how to fit into his life without people thinking he's gone crazy or amnesiac. That would be the best plan, fake amnesia from a small stroke, walk into an emergency room all confused, and have the docs and police help you ease into a strangers' life.

Even more exciting was to imagine jumping into a young woman's body, like Lila's. Finding out about what it's like to be a woman from the inside, to make love as a woman, to have babies and nurse them. Ben imagined that he wouldn't be bored for years. It would be the perfect way to avoid the whole shortness of life and complete unfairness of death. It seemed so wrong that you have only one life to live, and it's so short. Ben had so many things he wanted to do, and not enough time to do them. For years Ben had said that he wanted to live to be a hundred or more. It was shorthand for saying that he wanted to live out all of his potential, to live out all the lives he would like to live: be a scientist, and inventor, a mountain climber, an astronaut, an architect, a great lover, a painter, a musician, a bum, a criminal. He wanted to be all mankind, and womankind too.

The body jumper plot was so attractive to him because it was a form of immortality that included great variety. Ben didn't want to live forever, necessarily, but to live many times over, until he had exhausted all the possibilities that interested him. He felt a little guilty, afraid that deep down his work on life extension drugs was just a selfish desire to cheat his own individual death. He felt a little like a selfish child who can't understand why he can't have it all. He worried that his greedy envy of young people, his desire to hijack their lives, went far beyond a healthy zest for life, into a more predatory, vampiric realm. But then he told himself: Hey, it's just a fantasy.

5. Power Nerd

Back at his desk, eating lunch out of a cardboard container from the commissary, Ben reluctantly returned his wife Louise's call. She came up on his screen wearing what he privately called her "Power Nerd" filter: her brunette hair magically ungrayed and artfully tousled, an anachronistic mechanical pencil behind her ear, her eyes larger, darker and unbagged, her lips fuller and more shapely than they had ever been in reality, neck smooth and taut as it had been when they met in college thirty years ago, pens in a retro pocket protector in her jumpsuitish outfit.

She got right to the point: "Did they announce the bonus trips yet?"

"No, not yet."

"You've got to get us to Bali."

"You know it's entirely out of my control," Ben said.

"If they try to stick us in that crummy condo in Idaho again, with a bunch of lab techs and bean counters, I'm not going. You deserve to be in Bali with the execs."

"Louise, I go where they tell me. You know that. It's not like you can just buy a ticket and show up."

25

She frowned or grimaced or pulled some sort of face. It was hard to tell with the grooming filter flattening the wrinkles. Ben wished he could see her for real, deal with the older, un-filtered Louise. The gray hair, the little nanny goat flap of skin under her chin, the netted wrinkles around the eyes, the sunken bosom and heavier hips made her seem less formidable, at the same time that they turned him off and made their love mak-ing nearly a thing of the past. He felt more of a match with that Louise.

"Well," she said, "when are they going to announce the trips? I need to make plans here."

"Actually, I'm meeting with Kapoor right after lunch. If I get a chance, I'll ask him."

"If you get a chance? What does that mean? Just ask him, don't dance around it."

"It doesn't work like that. There's a tone and a style and rhythm to these things. It is a dance, and I don't get to lead."

She shook her head, sending pixels coruscating across her cheeks. Ben remembered how he had once been crazy about this woman, who now mostly irritated him. His libido was so low, and their bodies so old and familiar, that he rarely looked at Louise the same way he looked at Lila on the treadmill. He could still probably get it up for a hot younger woman, but the marital spark was gone. He fully understood why rich guys like Kapoor went after the young ones, found a trophy wife eager to trade her youth for security. And yet, given the unlikely op-portunity of his nailing Lila, he would probably turn her down. He'd rather both he and Louise were young again and full of champagne fizz, not flat like stale beer.

"Listen," Ben said, "I've got to get ready for my meet-ing. Can we talk about this tonight?"

"We're supposed to go to the lake tonight, remember? To see the guy about the retaining wall."

"I'm not sure we can afford to do all those repairs right now."

"You want the deck to fall in?"

"That's not what I'm saying. We might just have to wait a little bit, not do it all at once."

"You promised to meet this guy."

"Okay, I'll go straight to the lake from work. I'll meet you there."

Ben broke connection and set his handheld to voicemail so he wouldn't be interrupted. He rubbed his face and winced inside at the thought of disappointing Louise. Their chances of going to Bali were slim and getting slimmer. Likewise their chances of accomplishing all the deferred maintenance at the lake house.

6. Rolled Up in the Squeeze Down

The door to Trujib Kapoor's office was real wood, not glass or fiberplast like the doors on Ben's floor. He knocked and let his fingers linger on the polished grain.

"Come through," said a voice from within.

Ben stepped into the lair of a typical corporate babu. Genus Asiatica, species expatrius corruptus, an exotic transplanted to California. The elaborately carved cedar doorframe he touched in passing was from a Hindu temple, as were the brightly painted and gilded figures flanking the door. These and other spoils were the genuine articles, "rescued" by Kapoor's family from Poona during the riots following passage of the Secularization Act by the Indian parliament.

Behind a carved mahogany desk of colonial proportions, no computer screens in sight, Dr. Trujib Kapoor was reading from a sheaf of paper, looking down, pointedly ignoring Ben and making him wait.

Kapoor had the correct lineage for the corporate zeitgeist these days, being the second son of a family high in government and corporate service. Their influence spread coast to coast, from Mumbai-side in the west to Calcutta-side in the east. A couple of generations back, when the xenophobic pendulum in India had swung as close as it ever got to pluralism, his grandfather had "dipped into the saffron" and taken a Chinese wife, providing all-important blood ties to the mainland China economic powerhouse.

Kapoor had had the world handed to him. Rich parents in Bangalore, from one of the most prominent I.T. castes. Groomed for a tech berth from childhood, coached all through his undergrad and doctoral schooling, which his family underwrote by buying up all the stock options for every student loan he incurred. Started out in middle management for a biotech giant, switched to pharmaceuticals just before the nanotech bubble burst, avoiding becoming swamped along with his peers in the nanorecession, jumping into upper management under the boost of leveraged stock options.

Kapoor looked more like a prosperous Bangalore chip merchant than a corporate drone. His skin had a ruddy glow as if he had just stepped indoors from a sun drenched tropical marketplace. His pudgy bulk was draped with an old gold vest made of such a nubby, wrinkled hop sacking that it just had to be a Madras original. His was a conservative, old-school look: no tattoos, no piercing, no plating, no link or audio hardware clamped to his temples. But despite appearances, there was no doubt that Senior Research Executive Kapoor was firmly astride the tiger and Research Team Leader Ben Rasmussen wasn't.

All the big shots in the company were Asians of some kind. They came out of the "Benevolent Six," the super economies of Indonesia, Korea, Japan, China, Vietnam, and India—pejoratively and privately referred to by disgruntled Americans as the "Slant Six."

Dr. Kapoor finally looked up. "Ah…Dr. Rasmussen. Please be seated."

"Thank you." Ben sat on a low stool, real wood again and real uncomfortable.

"I trust you are well? And also your charming wife," his

eyes dipped to a concealed readout in the desk top, "Louise?"

"We're both fine, thank you," Ben replied. A little thread of alarm tugged at his guts. If Kapoor had called up his personnel file, it confirmed his fears that this was no casual conversation.

"Next year we will be implementing some adjustments and realignments of the main thrust of our research and development program," Kapoor said.

Ben squirmed. Why couldn't he just say there would be changes in R&D? Administrators never used one word when six would do. It was a common affectation, a triumph of style over content that eschewed abbreviations, initials, acronyms, and slang. High corporate discourse was meant to show that the wallahs had something important to say and all the time in the world to say it.

"As you know, perhaps better than most, the Rejuven human trials have not been encouraging."

"Well, it's still early days," Ben said. "I'm sure with a little tweaking we can get the same level of effect we achieved with animals."

"Unfortunately, the executive does not share your optimism."

The back of Ben's throat flooded with bile like lava from a volcanic vent. He almost wished Kapoor would return to his more circuitous style.

"What do you mean?"

Dr. Kapoor smiled. It was a very shallow smile, about a micron deep.

"Kalimer is cutting back on the Rejuvenator Complex project. We won't abandon chemicogenetic research entirely, but we would prefer to reallocate resources in favor of a more nano-technological approach to longevity."

"But nanotech is a dead end," Ben said. "I don't understand." He actually understood some things all too well. In the vernacular of Kalimer, "would prefer" meant that irrevocable decisions had been made at the highest level, and "reallocate resources" meant "we gonna fire people."

"Well, I wouldn't call it a dead end." Kapoor allowed his smile to spread wider and shallower. "However, when it comes to dead ends, I don't enjoy nearly your level of expertise and experience. Please enlighten me." Kapoor folded his hands expectantly, inviting Ben to expound, covering his hidden computer readout, and drawing attention to Ben's own history of dead ends over the years. It was a masterful put down.

Ignoring the insult, Ben plunged ahead. "Nanotech is just gadgeteering. It's nineteenth century mechanical engineering carried to its logical absurdity. Nobody's going to want to pump their bloodstream full of microscopic machines, even if they would work, which they won't."

"Surely you exaggerate. What about onboard dialysis for renal failure? What about pancrease synthesizer implants for cystic fibrosis?"

"Those are ninety-nine percent miniaturization. The nanotech components are very modest. I don't deny that a mechanical approach can help in treating a specific disease or deficiency. But to achieve a real extension of lifespan in a living system, you have to get down to the cellular and genetic level, and you have to use living agents."

Dr. Kapoor nodded without comment. Ben paused. Maybe this wasn't the time to rehash old arguments and entrench himself further in a losing position. He had the feeling that he was feverishly shoveling in a hole that might be already too deep.

"Sorry," Ben said, "I get carried away. You were explaining about a new emphasis for our research."

"Indeed." The smile faded. "I'm sorry to say that your team is being rolled up under Cynthia Lim. The duties of your position will be reduced and subsumed under hers."

A roll up was really a squeeze down. Cynthia was being demoted from junior admin to team leader, and Ben was being squeezed out like a watermelon seed between the administrative thumb above him and the forefinger of younger, brighter minds below him. An irrational hope flared briefly in his chest at the thought that they might actually lay him off rather than trade him or fire him for cause. A layoff would abrogate his student loans and grants, apply his paltry credits to the mortgages, and free him to seek other employment. With luck, he might break even.

Hope died as Dr. Kapoor continued. "Don't worry. We're not laying you off or firing you. We honor your many years of service and wish to keep you in the Kalimer family."

"I appreciate that," Ben said cautiously.

"We've gone to quite a bit of trouble to outsource your contract, rather than putting it out on waivers as we might with a less valued employee."

Ben secretly shuddered at the thought of being put on waivers. That meant that the highest bidder could buy out the remainder of his contract. His paper could be picked up by any-one. A friend of his had been put on waivers. One day he was happily splicing soybean genes for a prestigious Malaysian firm and the next day he was culturing sewage sludge bio-remedi-ators in the slums of Liverpool. And his friend was five years younger than Ben at the time.

Kapoor went on: "We've found you a nice spot with ChemGen, Ltd., at their home office in Kuala Lumpur. Kalimer has a small interest in their firm, so it's still in the family. They have graciously agreed to refinance your package at existing interest rates. The salary draw also remains the same."

"But isn't the cost of living in Kuala Lumpur much higher?"

"We all have to make sacrifices these days." Transla-tion: Take it or leave it. "We'd like you to finish up here before the end of the year, and report to ChemGen January fifth. I've arranged to have Personnel give you cash in lieu of your bonus trip to Idaho, so you'll have a little something extra to cover re-location." Translation: we don't want you poisoning the minds of the techs and bean counters in Idaho, much less the execs in Bali, and we won't pay moving expenses.

Ben clamped his lips together and looked down. His eyes stung and he felt like crying. He was being taken out of the only game worth playing, the only thing he was good at. ChemGen had no research division. They were a supplier of cut-rate viral cultures and standard tissue matrices. God knows what donkey work they'd have him doing. He felt like a sculptor with his arms cut off, a painter blinded, a knight captured and stripped of his sword. The fight against death would go forward without him, while he rotted in Kuala Lumpur. At ChemGen he'd never get to create anything new and important. He'd never have a chance to wipe out his subordinated debt and cash out ahead of the game, not if he stayed in harness there till he was ninety. Then there was Louise. She'd kill him. There was no way they could live in crowded, overpriced Kuala Lumpur in the style to which they were accustomed in Santa Rosa.

"Dr. Kapoor," Ben said, improvising desperately, "before we go down this road, I have to tell you that I'm on the verge of a real breakthrough. I just need a few more months, one more trial. I think perhaps it's not the RC12 formulation that's at fault, but the way Durance is implementing the protocol. If I could just visit them onsite and observe, I'm sure I could get a revamped trial on track. I might even salvage the current effort, if I could just work with the raw database."

"I'm sorry. The executive considers your recent requests for more personal involvement in the trials to be inappropriate. It is thought that perhaps you are already too close to the project, too deeply invested in a preconceived outcome. The UN Drug Authority has become very strict about our scientists meddling with the independent research contractors. We must avoid even the appearance of subjective bias. And you know that direct access to the raw data is against company policy. It would undermine the sovereignty of the Data Analysis Section."

Ben knew he was dead, but he couldn't give up. "I feel like I'm being shunted aside. I know my research is stalled, but surely that's no reason to junk it, especially in favor of some nanotech fantasy."

"Ben, I'm sorry, but it's really out of my hands. There are wheels within wheels here. You and I both are caught up in a system that sometimes seems heartless and irrational. I can only counsel you to keep faith, work hard, and persevere. No downturn lasts forever."

The platitudinous attempt at sympathy and mutuality was even more chilling than Kapoor's cheerful executioner manner.

Ben said, "I'm sorry too, but I don't see how this 'downturn' pinches your ass. It looks like I have no options here, so I'll take it like a good boy. But don't ask me to grin while I'm getting the shaft."

Kapoor abruptly dropped his mask of sympathy. "Listen," he said, "this is nothing like the shafting you probably deserve. Based on your record, you could have been dumped on the open market." He read openly from the readout cupped in his hands: "Second rate education at Stanford, paid for entirely by Kalimer; one patent for a viral marker no one has used in a decade; three ill-advised refinances of your original student loans, chasing other derivative patents that never earned back the risk capital; no significant publications since 2024. You've been coasting on salary draw ever since. Your slot on the rejuvenator team is a charity berth. You're lucky we found you a more-or-less lateral move into a company where we have some influence. If you don't show some gratitude and loyalty, you could still end up in the bachelor dorm of some white collar debtor's prison, or washing your own glassware in a clone clinic."

Ben stifled his rage. He mentally gathered his shell of distrust and caution around himself like armor. Kapoor's descent into direct speech was the most straightforward message he'd received from an executive in years. The threat was clear.

"Fine. I see what I have to do." He stood up and forced himself to bow slightly in farewell. "I'd better get back to my desk. I've got a lot of …finishing up to do."

Ben retreated, closing the real wood door ever so softly,

tenderly, while in his mind he slammed it so hard it brought the whole stinking building down in a pile of smoking rubble. He drifted downstairs, holding himself in a tight shell of control, keeping every movement smooth and slow and fluid. Inside the shell, the rubble of his dreams burned and settled, smoked and stank like death.

7. Back Door to the Orphanage

Back in his office, Ben stared at nothing, tasting ashes, smelling corruption, hearing groans and sirens just beyond the range of normal sound. He had been sitting there for half an hour, doing nothing, when Cynthia Lim's retro avatar appeared on his screen, big eyes, small mouth, tiny vampire fangs.

"I'm sorry," she said, so quietly he almost had to read her animated lips. "I didn't..."

Ben shook his head. "Not your fault. You're flattened too." This disaster was beyond the scope of her cunning or ambition. She was caught in the blast too, just a little farther from ground zero. Her connection with Kapoor had probably been enough to keep her in Santa Rosa, albeit with more work and less responsibility. With her at the helm, Rejuven was well and truly dead.

Cynthia said, "They want me to take over your projects. We'll need to talk."

Ben kept his tone businesslike. "I've got to update my files. I'll send you copies tonight and we can start going over them tomorrow."

"Okay." Her cartoon face added out.

His v-mail chimed with a reassignment notice from H.R., chimed again with details on whom to report to at Chem-Gen in Kuala Lumpur, chimed again with more papers to sign for H.R.

Ben left the v-mails for later and started mechanically opening and updating all his RC12 files. His supposedly secure data sectors opened without asking him for a password. All his passwords had been neutralized already. He tried to create a new a password and couldn't. Kapoor and H.R. were thorough, stripping him naked, not leaving him any secrets to hold hostage.

Ben wasn't worried about his superiors finding anything embarrassing in his database. He had learned from his friend, the soybean splicer who had been put on waivers, that nothing is private at work. His friend had also inspired Ben to take some elementary precautions. As Ben worked, tagging all the data he was supposed to send to Cynthia, he opened and closed every program and file he might want some day, after he left Kalimer.

He felt a rising panic deep inside, but pushed it down. While he still had access to Kalimer's system, he needed to work fast. Every little step he took, every breath he breathed might be crucial later on, so he wanted to get things right, right now. He put in an order for a full course of Rejuven, tailored to his age and gender and genome, to be delivered to his attention in Malaysia. He tagged it as a "quality control sample" and hoped that it would trickle through the bureaucratic channels unmolested. He activated Control Group Subject 240 in his database, an imaginary prisoner physically identical to himself, in a placebo control group cleared for later administration of Rejuven. Rejuven was his baby, and he wanted to leave himself a back door to the orphanage, just in case he needed it.

He finished by three o'clock and V-mailed Cynthia all the tagged data. He leaned back in his chair, pressing the palms of his hands into his eye sockets, willing himself to relax and wait until the hourly backup icon on his desktop stopped spinning.

He reached into the back of his bottom drawer and took out a battered, grimy plastic disk with "Dead" written on it in purple marker. It was his extra disaster backup, wireless, dense with data, anything but dead. He slid the slim plastic disk into

35

his pocket. It would take a really thorough sleuth from I.T. to tell that he had routinely made an extra backup of everything on his computer.

8. The Jetsons

In the basement of the Kalimer building, Ben caught the subway to the Sonoma County airport. He hiked out to his hangar and shoved up the door. His classic Sabreze waited in the shadows. He ran his eyes over her sleek carbon fiber lines, never tiring of looking at the beautiful white jet. He had built it himself over a period of five years. The first flight, ten years ago now, was still fresh in his mind as one of the peak moments in his life.

Ben went over the plane, the familiar steps of the pre-flight inspection calming him, making him feel for a few moments that his old familiar routine was still intact around him. But it didn't last. How would he get his plane and Louise's plane over to Kuala Lumpur? Were old timey homebuilts like theirs even legal in Indonesian airspace? Could he get the aviation grade alcohol the obsolete jet engines needed? He doubted it. He would go nuts if he had to leave the planes behind and couldn't fly.

The scope of the disaster was really sinking in. He pushed the jet outside and closed the hangar door. He stepped on the wing, swung a leg over the sill, and wormed into the cockpit, putting the plane on more than getting into it. He winced at the familiar pain in his back and hip. Starting the engine, he realized that all the pleasure had gone out of the familiar rituals. In a dead, quiet voice he announced on the radio, "Sabreze four niner papa, taxi from the T hangars to one eight right for left departure."

The map on the control panel screen showed five or six active planes on the ground and another half dozen in the air. But none of them had a "too close" halo, and the plane let him start taxiing to the runway. When he was lined up he pushed the throttle all the way forward. The little jet leaped forward and threw itself into the air.

Ben flew the plane himself for the takeoff, even though the autopilot could have done it better. He liked to do the take-offs and landings himself, to keep his hand in. But he was too depressed and worried to concentrate on flying all the way. Besides, it would be dark soon, there was a thick cloud deck to get through, and the wind was gusty. He punched in "LAKE" on the keypad and hit the autopilot key. Louise's recorded voice said in his earphone, "I've got it." Ben liked having his wife's voice as the plane's voice, rather than using one of the standard voices. It reminded him to fly safely so he could return to loved ones on the ground. He had recorded the messages in her plane in his voice.

The plane steadied, entered a climbing turn to the left, and settled on to the heading that would take him direct to Mono Lake. A mile to the south the setting sun glinted on Cotati Bay, the extension of San Francisco Bay created by the great quake of 2029, making the bedroom community of Rohnert Park an instant deep water port.

Ben leaned back in the reclined seat and closed his eyes. The plane climbed to 5,000 meters to avoid traffic in the Sacramento valley. It broke out of the clouds and flew on top in the last slanting rays of sunlight. The sun cast the shadow of the plane on a bank of dazzling white cloud, with a rainbow nimbus around it. Normally Ben would have taken control back for a while to play in the clouds, chasing his shadow and blasting in and out of cloud drifts. But he just didn't feel like it.

High above the clouds, he could think more clearly, dissect the traumatic interactions of the day and tease apart the motives of his adversaries. Perhaps Kapoor or some higher-up had been pulling subjects out of the prison trials to mask negative side effects of Rejuven. It's a classic tactic, almost a tradition in drug research. Ben wouldn't put up with that, so maybe Trudge was just getting him out of the picture. Maybe Cynthia

Lim wasn't really being demoted and saddled with extra work on a dying project, but rather put into line for the Rejuven bonuses that would have gone to Ben. Did she really seem sorry? How could you tell with that silly avatar?

Another thing: If they were giving up on the RC12 program, why had they just given it a corny consumer name and gone to the trouble and expense of formulating an oral dose and producing 30,000 units in retail packaging? Why push it even harder on the InMates show? It didn't make sense.

The sturdy little plane was slow—it would take over thirty minutes to travel the 250 miles to their Mono Lake house. But it was quiet and smooth and well automated. Ben had it wired so that he could have stood on the runway and flown the plane remotely if he wanted to, using his handheld, although it would have been illegal without a drone license.

With Precision Satellite Positioning, onboard collision avoidance, and transponder ID, Ben's plane could take him anywhere in North America, any time, without needing to file a flight plan or talk to anyone on the radio. But outside the Continental Free Flight Zone, there were more restrictions—permissions to request, controlled airspace to negotiate, flight plans to be filed, service fees to be paid, and so on. Kuala Lumpur was likely to have the same bureaucratic, centrally controlled system used in China and Japan, where individual flight was still an eccentricity of the wealthy and not within the grasp of motivated mid-levellers like Ben and Louise.

The plane sank back into the clouds, descending over the spine of the Sierras and slowing for its approach to the Mono Lake strip. The clouds thinned as he passed the divide and the jet popped out into the clear, sliding down the dry eastern slope of the mountains. This was about the only flight Ben and Louise took anymore, shuttling between their house in Santa Rosa and the cabin at Mono Lake. Sometimes Louise used her plane for a business trip to a far-flung reservoir or dam. She worked for WaterWorksInc. She had started with them when they were the California Water Resources Board, before it was privatized.

The plane lined up for a long final approach to the dry lake bottom strip. When Mono Lake finally dried up and the last of the "Save Mono Lake" fanatics died or drifted into the Arizona UFO camps, the water board opened the area for development. Louise was able to get them in on the ground floor of the new sky park, before the trendies ran the prices up.

How could Louise leave her job? She complained about the hours and the pay and the politics, but she loved messing about with her watershed computer models. Resource allocation was her religion. Next month WaterWorksInc was going to merge its Sacramento River operations with the corporation managing the San Joaquin watershed, gaining economies of scale to equal those enjoyed by Northwest H2O in the Columbia/Snake region up in Washington, Oregon, and Idaho.

The old lakebed made a perfect runway, over three miles long. Ben raised his hand to take over control, then dropped it. He just couldn't be bothered. The plane set itself down, braked, and turned off on taxiway Mary. It slowed to a stop and Louise said in his ear, "It's all yours."

Ben taxied over to their cabin and parked underneath in the shade hangar, next to Louise's pink jet. He sat for a moment, slumped in his seat, looking to the joke sign nailed to a post: "The Jetsons." Then he shook his head like a wet dog and forced himself to swing the canopy aside and get out.

9. Negative Calories

Upstairs, music was playing and Louise was sitting on the leather couch in the living room with the lights off, listening to a book and watching the light fade behind the cloud topped peaks to the west. She was dressed in a lime green micropore exercise jumper, her graying brown hair piled up behind her neck in a loose bun. The smart fabric firmed the loose skin on the backs of her upper arms and the cellulite on her thighs, but it couldn't disguise the bulges of her belly and hips. Ben was surprised that she was wearing such an unflattering outfit. Louise hated looking fat.

She looked up at him, smiled, and tapped her ear to turn off her book.

"Hi," she said, "How was work?"

Ben sighed and flung his vest over a chair. He sat down across from her. "Not so good. I'm afraid we won't be going to Bali."

"Oh Ben, not Idaho again. It's an insult." She rose and took a bottle of red wine off the piano.

"It's worse than that, I'm afraid. We're not going to Idaho either." Ben looked away. His eyes stung, his heart was pounding, and he felt sick to his stomach.

Louise said nothing, staring at him, her green eyes wide, cautious and disbelieving. She opened the wine bottle automatically, hardly looking at it.

"I couldn't believe it. I got in this morning and there was a summons from Kapoor, of all people." Ben began to tell the tale, forcing a hearty incredulity into his voice: Come laugh with me about this. As he got into his adventures with the V-mail and Cynthia Lim's weird behavior, Louise poured them wine and dumped a bag of chips into a crystal bowl on the coffee table between them, all without taking her eyes off Ben's face. He found it hard to meet her gaze. Her quiet attentiveness was scary. She seemed to be making mental notes of omissions and inconsistencies in his story, like a lawyer preparing her cross examination.

Ben was pretty sure he still loved his wife, but it was hard to tell. They lived under the same roofs, even slept in the same beds, but they seldom talked about anything and they hadn't made love for months. They alternated between ignoring and annoying each other.

When Ben got to the part about the RC12 program being

cut back, a pink flush rose from Louise's neck to her ears and into her cheeks. When he got to the news about Kuala Lumpur, she turned white again, quick as a panicked squid. She jumped up and turned on the light, as if to dispel the darkness Ben had brought into their home.

"No, that's crazy," she said. "I don't believe it."

"I'm afraid it's true. No doubt about it."

"We can't move to Kuala Lumpur. You'll just have to telecommute."

"No. They'd never go for that. I have to be there."

"Is it temporary? Some kind of field project? You go there and get them on track, then come back?"

Ben forced himself to look at her and speak calmly. "Louise, they sold my contract. It's not an assignment. It's a whole new job with a new company. It's permanent."

"But what about all our stuff? This place, the house, everything we've built up here?" She picked up a pillow off the couch and shook it at him, as if to say, what about this pillow? how can we live without this pillow? She threw it into his lap.

Ben put the pillow gently back into its place, and said, "We'll have some bonus money to move with, but things are bound to be very different over there." Ben had an image of them as a pair of orphan kittens, thrust into a harsh, alien environment. Both of them were California born and bred, members of the global community by position and class, but not by birth and nature. Although Ben worked for a multinational corporation, he had never lived anywhere but northern California.

"What about my job?" Louise asked. "It took me years to get into computer modeling. I'm fifty-five. At my age, I'll never get another job like this. How can you expect me to quit?"

Ben just looked down and shrugged, shaking his head slowly. He wanted to say do it for my sake, do it out of love, do it to stand by me. But he didn't feel enough love in his own heart to ask, and she no longer loved enough to offer. It was years too late. The boredom and routine and emptiness and just plain laziness of too many winters had eroded their love, like

41

rain washing sand out from under a roadbed until it hangs over nothing, looking whole and strong but merely waiting for the first unbearable weight to bring it crashing down.

"How can I just walk out on the whole bioregion?" she continued. She sat abruptly, grabbed a handful of chips, and stuffed a big one into her mouth. "We've got to combine three different water system models into one." It was hard to understand her, talking with her mouth full. "I'm in charge of converting the whole Russian River hydrological database to the tri-state standard. I have to see it through."

Ben sampled a chip himself. Ugh, they were Shrinkles, wafers of potato starch fried in denatured krill oil. Shrinkles contained a genetically engineered mirror image protein that gave them a rating of minus 300 calories per serving. Louise was really into the latest negative calorie diet foods.

"These are nasty," he said. "I'm sure they're not good for you. They make your breath smell like dirty socks."

Louise glared at him and stuffed another chip into her mouth. "I like 'em."

"Maybe you could telecommute," Ben said. "Most of your work is online."

"No way," she answered. "Only lightweights call in. I have to be here."

"Well, I have to be in Kuala Lumpur by January fifth."

"Thank god we don't have kids," she said. "This would be awful if we had kids in school." Her voice quavered and she looked away. She didn't want to cry but she probably would.

They had planned to have a daughter. They made the plan when they were both still in school. It was in the late teens and they believed in the "One Is Enough" campaign to cut greenhouse gases: one child, one dwelling, one car per family, planet wide, no exceptions. They bought an annuity package from Planned Parenthood for one child and put sperm and eggs on layaway. For a few years after graduation they made do with one car, one house, no plane. Then world temperatures cooled down and economies warmed up in the Soaring Twenties. They bought another car, then another house, then a plane to get there quickly, then a third car to leave at the lake, then two plane kits, and so on.

By the time they got around to having a kid, they were both forty-one. They couldn't afford the time and lost wages for Louise to carry the fetus herself, but they found a strapping Dutch refugee girl for a surrogate and implanted a daughter whose genome was ninety-seventh percentile across the board. She would have had green eyes like Louise and blond hair like Ben's mother and a compromise name of Marie Drew that both families could live with. But she died at birth of Multiple Environmental Insult. It was before they had the prenatal protocol for MEI, before they knew what to do with a newborn who was inexplicably allergic to everything.

Perhaps that's when Ben and Louise lost heart. They just stopped talking about kids, about themselves, about anything important, really.

"Maybe I could go on ahead and you could come later," Ben said, "after I make a place for us and you've had time to wind things up at work and, well, get used to the idea."

"I'll never get used to this idea," Louise said. "I wish you could quit."

"I can't. All my loans would come due. We'd lose everything."

"I can't believe you got us into this mess. You're supposed to be the big shot scientist, but you're such a child. You let them push you around."

"I'm sorry."

"You sure are." She said through tears. "I'm sorry too."

She put her wine glass down so hard the stem broke, but she didn't seem to notice. She stood and said, "I can't go down the drain with you. I just can't." She went into the bedroom and shut the door.

Ben watched a rivulet of red wine run to the edge of the table and start to drip on the white rug. He put his own glass on the floor to catch the drips, then stayed hunched over on the couch, staring at his dim reflection in the darkened window glass. We're like ghosts, he thought, spirits floating side by side, but not connected. Our love is too weak to hold us together anymore. The slightest breeze can blow us apart and we'll never find each other again in the dark. Won't even want to, won't even try.

He had always had trouble staying tuned into Louise and her life, especially when it required spending time on routine tasks like shopping for clothes or furniture together, giving foot rubs, cooking a dinner from scratch. And yet he knew those are the things that tend to root you in the present and deepen relationships. He found it hard to share his thoughts with Louise. It wasn't that he didn't trust her or love her. His thoughts often seemed banal or repetitive, boring, not worth sharing. As if it were the content that others wanted from him, when it was really the contact, the underlying message, like Vonnegut's Martian cave creatures who could only say two things to each other: "Here I am" and "Glad you are."

Ben was happiest when solving a problem. He loved to analyze the details of a problem, get down to basic principles, take something all apart and put it back together, predict what is not working and how to make a simple intervention that will get things working again. Nothing wrong with this impulse, it was the heart of him, his definition, the basis of how he fit into the world. The gadgety modern world needed repairmen, and Ben was a good one. But sometimes, he had to admit, there were problems he couldn't fix. Death was one. An unhappy spouse was another. Sometimes when Louise was sad, she just wanted a shoulder to cry on, not a fixit man.

10. Out of the Loop

Flying to work the next day, Ben flipped through his vmail. Lim wanted him to clear out his office today and somebody named

Chow at ChemGen wanted to know when he would arrive in Kuala Lumpur. Kalimer didn't like to linger over goodbyes. Just cut off the limb, cauterize, and forget about it. At least Chem-Gen seemed eager to have him start.

He switched to last night's episode of InMates L. He hated the InMates shows, but he couldn't stop watching them. He told himself he only watched because of his job, but really they aroused in him a stimulating anger, a pleasurable contempt for the marketing department, and a perverse pride in his connection to show business, however shoddy.

The characters' names were particularly annoying. In-Mates L starred lesbian women with names like Boobs, Li'l Piece, Sammy, and Haunch. The character names in InMates G and InMates T were just as bad, but he didn't watch them much.

Haunch was huddled on her bunk, crying. Sammy was comforting her, rubbing her back and brushing her lank blonde hair out of her runny mascara.

"If you want to get Boobs back," Sammy said, "you got to go on Rejuven. Boob looks amazing now. She could pass for forty, maybe thirty-five, so of course she's running with a younger crowd."

"I can't stand the needles," Haunch said, smearing her mascara even more.

Cut to Boobs in a sidebar, arms crossed, shaking her head, "Haunch is such a baby." She flips her red hair back and the camera lingers on her newly taut and shapely neck. She's fifty, the same age as her girlfriend Haunch, but she looks ten or fifteen years younger. Ben wondered whether that was her real neck and chest or a torso double.

Boobs went on: "Haunch is fifty years old and she cries like a baby about getting a shot? If she really loved me, she'd be on Rejuven like the rest of us. I'm sorry, but she's getting left behind, and it's her fault, not mine."

Cut back to Haunch and Sammy on the bunk. Sammy said, "No more needles. They got pills now. You need to get on the Rejuven right away."

Ben turned the show off. They weren't wasting time getting the new name and formulation into the plot line. How long did it take for a new formulation to make it out of R&D animal trials, get the FDA rubber stamp for human trials, brief the marketeers, and get the InMates writers on board? Several months, anyway. And he had no clue until yesterday. He was farther out of the loop than he ever imagined.

Part Two

11. Kicking the Mountain

Curled in the coach class seat of an ancient 787 bound for Kuala Lumpur International Airport, Ben is deep in a dream. He is ten years old, helping his father restore the old 1969 Datsun. The fenders and hood are off the 240Z and his dad is straddling the exposed engine, spraying ether into the dual SU carburetors.

"Okay, turn 'er over Benny."

Ben twists the slim silver key in the ignition. He hears the engine turn over, chug...chug...chug, jiggling his seat. He can smell the ether and the dusty motor oil smell of the old car.

"Okay, hold it." Dad gives each carb's mixture nut a slight turn with a wrench. "Try 'er again."

Ben cranks the engine again, but it doesn't start. Now it sounds like someone choking, "cough...cough...cough."

He looks through the smeared windshield and his father is trying to pour water into his mother's slack mouth. She is choking and coughing.

Then Ben himself is at her bedside, in the tiny nursing home room he visited on breaks from college. "Mom, it's Ben," he says, "your son."

She just lies there, scanning his face with her watery blue eyes without recognition. He twists the key sticking out of her sternum and she coughs, coughs again, and closes her eyes, perfectly still. He knows she is dead and he can't start her up again, and it's all his fault.

Ben woke up feeling panicked, powerless, and guilty. Then he realized it was just a dream. He was relieved but disoriented for a moment. He thought he could still smell the ether, but it was just the over-conditioned, stale air of the 787. They were announcing something over the PA that he couldn't understand. The note of the jet's roaring engines descended a half tone and the plane banked sharply, probably starting their descent toward KUL, Kuala Lumpur International Airport.

After his mom died, his dad stopped driving the Datsun, let it collect dust in the garage. Ben used to go and just sit in the car sometimes, smelling that smell, remembering better times. It was his childhood dream to drive that sleek blue sports car one day. He never did drive it, but he rode in it many times as a kid, always alone with his dad because it only had two seats and mom hated driving it. It was stiff, bouncy, noisy ride that always felt fast even at the speed limit. It was so much more exciting than the family minivan. On Sunday mornings when his mom and sister went to church, his dad and he would go to the garage. Ben handed him tools, sorted the sockets by size, cleaned parts in a coffee can of degreaser and put them in zip lock bags, label the bags with a Sharpie marker. They had coffee back then, before the blight. They had degreaser that actually dissolved grease instead of just making it smell like oranges. They had Sharpies that would write on anything, before all those carcinogens were banned.

Ben ran through a familiar calculation: Mom died at sixty, Dad died at sixty-two, I have two years left. He had the same genetic markers for heart disease that his dad had. His had remained switched off till now, but he was keeping a close eye on his genome. His chance of Alzheimer's was slimmer, and they could mostly manage it now, but he still panicked every time he forgot the name of some starlet or well known CEO. Coming from short-lived stock had a lot to do with Ben's choice of research specialty. Going with Kalimer in the first place was always about extending his own life and helping others live longer. It looked like he was too far outside Kalimer now to accomplish his dream.

It really didn't bear thinking about anyway. It was probably all a lie, or two lies really. The first lie was that he could

50

save the world, when he really just wanted to save himself from death, or from having to deal with the fact of death by postponing it. Looking at the proposition objectively, saving the world couldn't be done by prolonging life, because there are already too many people. But perhaps if people didn't fear death so much, they might not have so many kids, trying desperately to cheat death by continuing on in their children. He suspected that it didn't really make sense. Who thinks about immortality or overpopulation when they're eighteen and turned on to someone? You just do what your body wants you to do and oops, we're pregnant, I guess we're having a kid. The biological imperative was so much stronger than Ben's vague utopian fantasies. He was really just a guy afraid of dying, and stupidly resentful about mortality. He'd dedicated his life to kicking the mountain, to running repeatedly headfirst into the same brick wall.

The second lie was thinking that anything he did as an employee of a drug company would benefit anyone other than the shareholders. Any benefit to humanity would be a side effect of increasing profit for Kalimer.

12. Not for Human Consumption

"Welcome to Hilton Tower," the desk clerk said. She looked like a runway model with a perfect figure and daring décolletage, but in miniature, the whole package topping out at about 1.6 meters. Ben forced a smile and waved his handheld at her terminal. It beeped and she said, "Yes Mr. Rasmussen, I have your reservation. And a package for you. Your room is 21286." She handed him a key card and a cardboard box.

"What floor is that?" Ben asked.

"Two hundred and twelve. The express elevators are to your right."

"What's the deviation up there?"

"Plus or minus six meters."

"Do people get cloud sick?"

"Oh no, you won't even feel it."

She was wrong. When Ben was in his room, he felt a distinct movement. Not queasy-making for him, thank goodness, like in a boat. There was no up and down component. But he could definitely feel himself changing direction about every four seconds, as the building swayed in the afternoon wind. Hilton Towers was a 1,200 meter cloudscraper. Back in the forties it had been the tallest building in the world for six days, and the tallest building in Malaysia for nearly six months. It was designed to move in wind and earthquakes, vibrating like a cello string in complex harmonics, generating a significant amount of power from it's piezoelectric transductive skeleton.

The package was from Kalimer Quality Control. It contained his shipment of the new Rejuven capsule formula—six randomly selected bottles of thirty capsules each, labeled "Property of Kalimer Pharmaceuticals. Not for human consumption." He stashed the bottles in his suitcase. When he was established at ChemGen, he'd find a way to analyze the capsules.

Ben collapsed on the bed in his clothes and let the tidal sway of the tower lull him to sleep. He only intended to have a brief nap, but when he woke it was full dark outside and he couldn't even remember what day it was. His handheld told him it was four in the morning. He had to report to his first day of work at ChemGen at nine, so that left him plenty of time to shower, get breakfast, and find his new workplace.

Satisfied with this plan, Ben fell back to sleep and awoke in a panic at eight AM.

13. New Leper in Town

Jetlagged and heat stroked, with swollen feet and sore knees, Ben spent his first hours at ChemGen with a personnel officer named Ulang, who called himself a Protocol Liaison. Ulang was about four feet tall, a perfect miniature of the corporate mandarin, wearing a raw silk overvest in perfectly neutral gray, with capped and flared shoulders that Ben said reminded him of the roofs of Chinese temples.

Ulang didn't appreciate the temple comparison.

"You must avoid any mention of religion here," he said. "Religious harassment is cause for dismissal. Be careful that your coworkers never hear you refer to temples, churches, or deities such as Allah, Jaweh, or Jesus, pardon my language."

Ben had observed metaphysical correctness in the states, but he wasn't prepared for the strictness of its application in Malaysia. Here he must avoid any mention of the theological or supernatural. In the east they still remembered the right wing religious regimes and fundamentalist terror parties that had been swept away by global economic reform. Reformed "progressive" governments now ruled in the Benevolent Six countries, based on the Global Monetary Fund's principles of fiscal responsibility that placed the profit motive above all else. This climate allowed the multinational corporations to successfully lobby for sweeping secularization laws. In K.L. a simple "insha'Allah" was tantamount to terrorism.

All the holidays in his three hundred page employee manual were secular in nature. Religion survived among the elderly, the unmedicated insane, or disaffected and disenfranchised youth who practiced a sort of virtual mysticism on the net, enhanced by links and drugs.

For all his metaphysical correctness, Ulang wasn't above identifying those they passed in the halls by name, rank, and religious leanings: "That was Mr. Darkoosian, in charge of purchasing, a missionary Dutch Christian…Ms. Fatima Binte Omar, Data Analysis, Muslim…Mr. Rishka Santabong, Organics Production, Hindu…Al Henderson, Plant Services, Ethical Atheist, née Baptist."

"Who is my immediate superior?" Ben asked.

"Ms. C. F. Chow, Head of Synthetic Procurement."

"And what is her religious affiliation, which we are never to mention?"

"That is for Ms. Chow to say."

"And what exactly is Synthetic Procurement?"

"That also is for Ms. Chow to say." Ben thought it curious that Ulang would be so gossipy about everyone but this Chow person. He decided to wait until the tour was over and talk to Chow herself. But the tour didn't exactly end. The personnel guy dumped him in the employee lounge, saying "You may recreate here while I perform an errand. I will return in ten minutes."

Ben sat down in a plastic chair and looked around. There were six or seven people fixing chox, getting snacks from a machine, or chatting in English and Malay at small tables. He sat at a table alone, smiling shyly and trying to make eye contact so he could nod pleasantly and perhaps introduce himself. Nobody would look at him. He sensed sidelong glances, but when he turned his head, the person would look away and pretend to be engrossed in the fractal pattern of the plastic tabletop. Within two minutes, everyone had completed their tasks or picked up their cups and napkins and left. It was like he had some unmentionable respiratory plague.

His guide didn't return by the end of the workday. Ben sat in the lounge for two hours, mostly alone. When people entered and saw him, they quickly grabbed snacks and left. He killed the time going through the 300-page employee manual, drawing up an annotated organization chart, trying to figure out the power structure and the status of the people he'd met so far.

The next day he learned why he was a leper. In the course of signing new subordinated indenture papers in the personnel office, his compensation counselor told him, "You can keep your retirement loan account in Kalimer stock, if you wish. Since they took us over, we have daily adjusted stock parity."

Ben didn't want to appear ignorant, so he kept still. But he was shocked with surprise. According to Kapoor back in the states, Kalimer had a small interest in ChemGen. Now it appeared that they had a controlling interest. Some things began to make sense. People were leery of him because he came from the new owners. They had no idea he was demoted in disgrace. They probably thought he was advance man for the exorcists, infiltrated to identify the malcontents, slackers, and overcompensated drones who would be sacrificed in the downsizing ritual of corporate merger. They must figure him for a Kalimer spy at the very least. That would explain why no one wanted to talk to him or even be in the same room with him if they could help it. They were scared.

14. Boom Town on the Boil

For Ben, Malaysia was one long fever dream. Kuala Lumpur was a boom town on the boil, a seething stew of Malay indigenes, Chinese and Korean commie-capitalists, and Indian bureaucrats. The mix was seasoned with an overgenerous sprinkling of Aussies, Brits, Yankees, and other Anglo hangers-on. This polyglot mob poured out over the soft tar of freshly paved streets in electric trishaws, solar bikes, propane minibuses and articulated Great Wall limos. Glittering latticework cloud scrapers soared 300 stories high. On the sidewalks below, deformed children begged for UN dollars.

This was what they called the dry season, but it rained every day. Promptly at fourteen o'clock the muggy atmosphere between the cloudscrapers thickened, turned black, and flushed a waterfall down on a suddenly blooming crop of pastel umbrellas. The humidity rose from ninety to a hundred percent and the temperature dropped a paltry ten degrees, down to thirty degrees centigrade. At fourteen forty-five the downpour shut off like a faucet and the insistent sun reappeared.

The tropical climate was the worst part of the city Ben was learning to call "K.L." Stepping outdoors was like being buried in steaming hot towels, a tangible weight upon the skin that made him pop out in sweat all over. Indoors the icy air conditioning dried the sweat to clammy shivers. Shifting from one extreme to another had given him a constant sore throat, sinus headache, and post nasal drip. On the other hand, his arthritis liked the heat. His hands and knees felt almost normal.

He sniffed as he peered through the dashboard of his cheap electric rental, a bright pink Malacca Sprint that could barely proceed at a jog. Rain sheeted off the windscreen, defeating the wipers. He was looking for 524 Jaibar Street. Every time he queried the car's map, it said "Turn left next intersection." He was sweating in the car because the air conditioning didn't work right. Whenever he turned it up to high, a tinny voice said from the dash, "Warning, high rate of discharge. Range at this current draw is eighty-six kilometers." The message repeated every ten seconds as long as the AC was set on high. It was less annoying to just leave it on low and sweat.

After describing two full circles around a huge irregular block, Ben grabbed a fortuitous parking place and got out to proceed on foot. The rain was letting up but he took his lavender blue umbrella anyway. He had learned that much.

Jaibar street turned out to be a covered alley so narrow he had mistaken it twice for a doorway. Between a noodle shop and a scar parlor was the glass door of 524. Taped to the inside of the door was a card, dotting with icons and scan blocks, with one small line of actual text reading, "Abdor bin Ahmad, Rental Agent." Abdor was the cousin of the brother-in-law of the personnel director's assistant at ChemGen. Their idea of employee housing assistance had proved dim and convoluted.

The door was locked. He knocked and waited. He hoped this lead was not another dead end. Three weeks earlier he had started looking for a house. Last week he lowered his expectations to a semi-D or a flat. Today he hoped to nail down the two bedroom apartment that Abdor was rumored to have available. Housing was very tight in K.L. He couldn't afford anything nearly as nice as his and Louise's place in Santa Rosa or even their little condo/cabin at Mono Lake. Especially since they were still paying on both places. Louise was supposed to put the houses on the market and come over to join him, but every time they talked she had a new reason for delay. Ben had tried to prepare her for the situation in Kuala Lumpur. Prices were high. As a foreigner on a work visa, he wasn't paid as much as an Asian and didn't qualify for government housing subsidies.

He knocked again. No one was in sight, but there were lights on inside. He couldn't hear anything over the roar of traffic from the main road. He mopped his forehead with the handkerchief he had learned to carry, and decided to count slowly to seventeen, then knock again.

A short figure appeared in the office within and walked slowly to the door. He was wearing a white short sleeved shirt, a white felt cap, gray jeans and rubber sandals. His wrinkled face had the color and sheen of lacquered mahogany. He unlocked the door and let Ben in. It was cold inside. Ben sneezed.

"Is this the rental agency?" Ben asked

The man replied in what sounded like Malay.

"Just a moment," Ben said, holding up his handheld and punching up his translation program. With a finger on the English-to-Malay button, he repeated, "Are you the rental agent?" then lifted his finger to release a string of bubbling Malay syllables from the handheld's speaker.

As the small man replied, Ben held down the Malay-to-English button, and his handheld said, "This young man, one Abdor bin Ahmad by name, is indeed the housing pimp."

It was a cheap program, downloaded free at the car

rental counter. Supposedly it made you fluent in Malay, bazaar Mandarin, Hindi or Tamil. Unfortunately, many things could defeat the idiot savant software--high ambient sounds, unusual accents, fast talking, or literally translated idioms.

According to the net summary, everybody in K.L. understood English and most spoke some as well. But you'd never know it. Ben suspected that many of the natives he encountered were only pretending not to understand English, just to annoy him and remind him that he didn't belong here. He resolved to make the best of the kludgy software.

"Miss Ngumo at the ChemGen personnel office said you might know of a two bedroom apartment for rent."

"Oh, one cannot rent just the bedrooms, also must rent the kitchen, the drawing room, and the slaughterhouse."

Ben had no idea what the correct translation for "slaughterhouse" was, but he focused on the essentials. "Yes, I want to rent the whole apartment. Where is it?"

"Is not far. If my confused uncle will just follow me."

He led Ben out the door and up the alley. He hailed a tri-shaw, a spidery buggy with narrow seating for two on top of the batteries. The driver stood over the rear wheel, behind the seat, gripping the steering bar and peering over the passengers' heads.

"I have a rental car we can take," Ben said, holding the translator speaker close to Abdor's ear so he could hear over the traffic noises.

"No need to rent a car," Abdor answered, "taxi can go cheaper."

Ben shrugged and climbed up into the seat. They set off with a hum like a five hundred pound mosquito, splashing through the puddles and dodging traffic. Remnants of rain blew sideways into Ben's face, evading the skimpy awning of solar collector cloth over the passenger seat.

They got out at a high stucco wall with an arched opening. Abdor unlocked the wrought iron gate in the arch, leaving Ben to pay the fare. Like everything in K.L., it was exorbitant—

as much as he'd spend for lunch back home.

Within the walls was a square of ruined garden with several packing crate shelters built around shattered tree trunks. An old woman was filling a plastic bottle with rusty water from a tap at the base of a dry fountain. Beyond the fountain were wide steps leading up to a three story white stucco building whose colonial symmetry had been compromised by a post modern facelift sometime in the last century.

Abdor said something, directing his remarks to Ben's handheld. Ben keyed the translator and heard, "This building was once an orphanage perpetrated by Catholic devil nuns." Abdor smiled. "No more god here now. Can be first class dwelling for homeless foreign gentleman."

They went into the lobby of the building. A huge rubber tree that had cracked the pot it was planted in reached up a stairwell to a dusty skylight three stories above. Silver mailboxes were nailed to the wall and a bulletin board carried notes in several scripts, icons, and languages, including English: "Residents shall not thro garbage out the windoes."

The stairs were partially blocked by a teenage Chinese girl with an orange plastic clipboard. She was sitting in a student writing desk just like the ones Ben had used at Stanford. Around the girl's neck was a chain and hanging from the chain was a machine pistol with its plastic stock taped together and the flat black paint rubbed shiny on the stamped tin of the magazine. It was covered with band stickers.

Ben stopped short when he saw the gun. Abdor turned back to him, a wide grin revealing a gold incisor with a ruby chip inset. "Very high security building," he said, "very safe here."

Ben eyed the antique slug thrower with dismay. He tried to imagine his wife coming home to an apartment where she had to sign in with a schoolgirl terrorist. In his mind a dark corner he had been avoiding grew too light to ignore, and he understood what people meant when they talked about "dawning awareness." He saw then what he had been unable or unwilling to see earlier: that Louise might never join him in Malaysia. It was not just too far from home. It was too different and too frightening.

Abdor was explaining to the handheld, "Is best to give guards fifty or sixty ringgit or a UN dollar from this time to that time. Good tippings make good service, so they not strip naked your visitors. Unless the gentleman so desires."

"I think I'd prefer to do my own strip searching."

"Exactly so. More discretion. Unfortunate that most apartments now using these cheap Chinese girls, on account of rich orphan resource in labor market."

After several garbled exchanges, Ben understood that in local Chinese families, two boys were born for every girl, and many Chinese girl babies were put up for adoption by Malays. The Malays set the girls out at child labor until puberty, then put them to work as prostitutes or host mothers for more Chinese baby boys. Ben closed his eyes and leaned against the wall for a moment. He felt like a child out in the real world for the first time. He wanted to retreat, to go all the way back to the womb or at least as far as California. He longed for the simple and familiar pleasures he had taken for granted and now seemed so far away and dreamlike.

Abdor signed the girl's clipboard and led Ben upstairs. They climbed worn red tile stairs with a brand new aluminum handrail. Ben huffed and puffed in the muggy air and had to rest halfway up. The stairwell walls were covered with spray painted graffiti in some kind of Arabic looking script. Ben asked what it said.

"This ignorant one lacks that knowledge," Abdor replied. "Cannot read the Jawi writing. Bad mullah boys maybe write 'There is no god but Allah,' or rude talk like that."

From a ChemGen orientation pamphlet, issued to all expats, Ben had heard that since the wave of secularization laws in Asia, public religious expression was illegal and considered vulgar. The laws forbid organized religions to run schools, fund orphanages, or minister to the poor. Such enterprises were considered "metaphysically incorrect forms of institutionalized proselytizing."

Abdor led him to the third floor, where he opened two locks on a steel door textured to look like wood. He bumped the door open with his shoulder and motioned Ben in. The apartment was cooler than the hall, but stuffy and smelled of mold, cat pee, and curry. The front door opened directly into the kitchen. Two walls embraced a prefab corner module of stark utilitarian plastic in a sickly shade of mustard yellow.

Abdor poked at a keypad on the wall near the door. Lights came on, heat pumps shifted to high speed, and the opening discords of Schrader's Concerto in D drifted into the dank air.

"This floor was once the girls' dormitory," Abdor said, "remodeled from deflowering of virgin martyrs to modern conveniences of domestic bliss."

A long, narrow, high ceiling room had been hacked into a shotgun flat. The kitchen, living room, two bedrooms, and bath were all in a line like train cars, with the connecting doors lined up to give a depressingly short view the length of the apartment. Ben thought you could fit all five rooms into the living and dining area of his old house. You had to go through both bedrooms to get to the bath.

Abdor pointed proudly to the new partition walls. "All new constructions, finest recycled materials."

The new walls were rough gray and didn't match the old plaster walls at all. In one corner the plastic lattice studs showed through the thin layer of foamcrete. An over-spray of gritty gray foamcrete was splattered over crown moldings and window panes. It was like the girls' dorm had been colonized by a giant paper wasp that secreted its series of brood chambers in an instinctive pattern completely alien to the larger cavity's original purpose.

Abdor gestured vaguely around him. "Compact floor plan for living in turn. Ample space for the storage."

Ben didn't bother replying. It was too much trouble to fool with the translation program. He peered into a small closet

set into the corner of a bedroom. Green mildew speckled the back wall and shelf fungus grew on the baseboard. He went on to the bathroom, where a cockroach the size of his thumb had drowned in the toilet and a green lizard clung to the wall. He massaged the bridge of his nose. He felt like crying. He was too old and tired for this.

Abdor stuck his head into the bathroom. "All new fixtures in the slaughterhouse." He lured Ben back into the bedroom by throwing open a window shutter and letting in a blinding shaft of light.

"Free natural light, or one can also petition the power. Wonderful view of the K.L. profile."

Ben glanced out the window at the view of grimy plastic dumpsters, a tent pitched up against the rear courtyard wall. and a few nondescript buildings beyond.

"It seems a little small," he said.

"Perhaps can appreciate altitude of ceiling."

"Perhaps can tell me how much the rent is?"

"For revered associate of ChemGen, only six thousand UN dollars this month. Next month adjusted for the inflation."

"Jesus Christ, that's half my salary."

Abdor frowned and folded his mahogany arms. "There is certainly no need to swear," he said softly, in perfectly clear English. "May this humble rental agent inform the homeless foreigner that the Chinese girl who guards the lobby pays eighty percent of her salary to share a tent in the garden?"

"Sorry," Ben said. "What I mean is, you don't have anything larger in this price range?"

Abdor unfolded his arms to shrug, empty palms upwards, returning to sing-song Malay, "Indeed, is best cat in very small litter."

"Smells like cat too," Ben said. "I'll take it."

15. Uninformed Consent

It took him four days to track down Harriet Chow, his new boss. As soon as he saw her, he thought, "Dog Chow," and privately bet that was her nickname at work. She looked like a pug dog, complete with wattles, double chins, hairy ears and moist nose. In her retro black pajamas and wrinkled Dacron overvest, she might have stepped out of one of those kitsch holos of dogs dressed in human clothes, playing cards or shooting pool.

"I am Synthetic Procurement of Raw Ingredients," she said, "Some I buy, some I get from animal farm in country, some I get from clinics, some I want you make in lab."

"What do you want me to synthesize in the lab?"

"We soon need much fetal stem cells, amniopeptin, protein90." Chow stuck a sheaf of paper in Ben's face. "Production quotas next quarter."

Ben felt his eyebrows rise and his eyes widen before he regained control of his reaction. He was familiar with all three ingredients--they were used in Rejuven. The fetal stem cells were tweaked to encourage production of deficient cell types in older people, especially brain neurons and sex hormones. The amniopeptin was an immune enhancer. Heat shock protein was used to make augmented telomerase, the cellular clock re-setter in Rejuven. If Kalimer was giving up on Rejuven, why was their newly acquired subsidiary gearing up to produce more of some of the drug's key components?

Ben scanned the columns of figures.

"This is very...ambitious," he said, "I doubt that all your lab space, working around the clock, could produce the heat shock protein alone, much less all three."

"Oh no," Chow chuckled, her chins bobbing, "you need synthesize only ten percent. Rest we harvest in our clinics."

"Then why synthesize any?"

"We blend ten percent synthesized material, ninety percent human harvested, and Malaysian law say we can label all as "synthesized." That how Kalimer want it. They want call their drugs 'all synthetic', not from human."

That seemed to confirm his suspicion that much of the production was destined for Kalimer. And it gave him a queasy feeling. He had always assumed that the Malaysian components of Rejuven were 100% cultured in a lab, as advertised.

"Have you always done it this way?"

"Oh, yes. Harvested human tissue very good, very safe. But Americans and Euros so superstitious. They worry too much about viral contamination and human rights. Better they do not see 'harvested' on label."

"I understand." Ben said, but he didn't really understand what was going on. Ramping up to produce vast amounts of these ingredients only made sense if Kalimer were going ahead with Rejuven and had placed orders for commercial quantities of its ingredients.

He needed to find out more. "I need to see the whole operation, clinics and all. So I can see where I fit in."

Ordinarily this would violate the corporate "need to know" caste system that kept people isolated in their narrow job descriptions. But his status as suspected Kalimer spy gave him some leeway. Chow hid her objections behind a blank doggy stare.

"Very well," she said, "we visit farm some day, clinic some day."

"Is there a clinic in K.L.?"

"Eight clinics in K.L."

"Show me one tomorrow."

She smiled and nodded curtly. But her glaring eyes made her look like a pug that wished it was a Doberman that could rip his throat out.

The next day they visited the Lotus Foundation's Genetic Health Clinic #34, in a strip mall by the airport. From his orientation packet, Ben knew that the Lotus Foundation was a subsidiary of ChemGen. Nothing identified the clinic as wholly owned and operated by ChemGen. In fact, it wasn't even identified as a clinic. The sign said "Body Beautiful" and the décor and furnishings of the clinic were more like a beauty salon. It was next door to a lingerie boutique. In fact, you could enter the clinic from the boutique, between the bustiers and the garter belts.

In the brightly lit waiting room, six young girls sat on fuchsia cushions on the floor, thumbing holo magazines and chewing gum in time to piped-in gamelan sambabong music. Chow led Ben through a door marked "Please wait to be seated" in six languages, into a huge room divided into treatment cubicles. Each cube was tricked out like a beauty parlor, with expansive mirrors, shelves of cosmetic samples, chox dispensers, potted plants, and link sets. Automated surgical tables were disguised as reclining salon chairs, with glitter plush upholstery and gold plated stirrups. A dozen more young girls sat bored and restless, waited on by brisk medtechs in orange smocks who bustled from cube to cube, adjusting diagnostic cuffs, monitoring neural blocks, and drawing the curtains on each cube for the five painless minutes it took for the automated chairs to scrape and suck their riders.

The air was heavy with competing scents of gardenia, musk, vanilla, and patchouli. Underneath was the faintest hint of blood, sex, and alcohol.

"This is harvest floor," Chow explained. "Girl can be screened, typed, treated, discharged in optimal twenty-three minutes. Even real busy, nobody wait more than one hour, tops."

She led him through an unmarked door. "This is threshing lab," she said, turning on a light. "All automated. All harvested raw material pumped in here and processed." She circled the room, pointing out centrifuges, viral filters and other black boxes connected with plastic piping. It looked like a refinery, only very clean and in miniature.

Ben lagged behind, feeling sick. He didn't really listen as Chow explained in avid detail how the threshing process separated the various proteins, blood fractions, fetal stem cells, and "impurities." He didn't ask what the impurities were, but he could imagine. The surgery bots were the descendants of machines first left behind by medical missionaries in the Twenties and Thirties. They had the apps for tumor removal, harvesting eggs, tying tubes, therapeutic abortions—whatever you chose from the menu. The machines worked quickly, efficiently, and well; it was the machinery of ethical oversight and informed consent that had broken down in the Forties. Ben had no conscious belief in life after death, especially for fetuses, but he imagined that in the background susurrus of the machines he could hear the dying Doppler screams of unborn souls streaming toward the final light.

16. In the Slaughterhouse

Ben was relieved after his credit check came up green and he got the key card for his new apartment. It was a dump, a real step down. But it was his dump, and even a step down was a step closer to getting settled so that Louise could join him. Might join him.

He checked out of his hotel and bought a double air mattress, bedding, towels, chox and a chox pot. In his new apartment he dumped everything on the floor, got out his handheld and called Louise. She punched up live, wearing a slate jumpsuit and an umber silk overvest. She looked startled when she saw it was him. Behind her he saw the yellow walls of the living room of the Mono Lake house, and Ben wondered why she would be so dressed up at the lake.

He started to tell her about the new apartment. "I'm in it now, just got the key," he said.

"Why don't you show me," she asked.

"All right, sure," Ben replied, although he really wanted a little more time to soften her up before showing her the apartment. He reversed the lens on the handheld and let her see the living room. He walked slowly through the string of empty rooms, panning the handheld and narrating as he went: "It's like living on a train—the Orient Express."

"Just what I always wanted," Louise said from a small widow in the corner of the screen, "to live on a train. It's awfully small."

"Our landlord says we should appreciate the altitude of the ceiling." Ben sat down again on the floor.

Louise grimaced. "We haven't had a landlord since we were in school."

"Well, I realize it isn't much, but it's a start. It will look better when we get some furniture. You can pick whatever you want. I'll wait till you get here."

"I need to talk to you about that," she said

"Good, let's make a plan. Have we got any offers on the houses?" Ben cradled the screen in his lap, wishing he could cradle his wife in person. Louse gazed up at him, her dark eyes shining. With tears?

"I've tried and tried to get used to the idea of moving," she said,. "but I just can't. I can't live there." She started to cry. "It's not the apartment. It's…it's…" She reached forward automatically to key in a grooming mask. She never liked him to see her crying. Her features became more symmetrical, her lips and cheeks rosier, her eyes darker and free of tears.

Ben looked down at the false image of his wife in his arms. "Louise, I realize this is a step down for us. I know it's a very strange place, but I think we can get used to it. I'm getting used to it." That's a lie, he thought.

"I don't want to get used to it. There's nothing for me to do there. No job, no friends." Her face became stiffer, more formal as she adjusted the grooming program to map her features more loosely. It was like talking to an oil painting. "I'm just too old and settled to move halfway around the world."

"Couldn't you just come out for a couple of weeks and see how you like it?"

"Please don't ask me again. It just makes it harder."

"But what are you going to do? I don't want to live apart for who knows how long."

"I've made up my mind about something and I'm having a really hard time telling you. I got an offer for a promotion at work, in charge of a new project, and I accepted it. I'm going to stay here, by myself."

"That's okay," Ben said. "I can see you have to finish your projects." He felt relieved. For a moment there, he had feared she was leaving him. "How long will the project take?" "That's not the hard thing," she said, shaking her head. "The hard thing is I'm leaving you."

Ben felt as if someone had punched him in the stomach. He couldn't breathe out, couldn't breathe in. finally he got some air and said, "I'll come back as soon as I can. We'll talk about it in person."

"No, I've filed for divorce."

Ben grabbed the screen so hard the plastic flexed, trying to choke off her words. Her image shifted to the stylized caricature she used on the phone when talking to strangers.

"All you have to do is log on to public records and con firm it," the cartoon continued.   "I hope you won't fight me on this. It's for the best."
Ben could only shake his head. His throat closed up and two hot tears leaked out of his eyes and splashed on the screen.

"It will go through uncontested as soon as you log on and file." She said. "I hope you will forgive me. I just can't uproot from everything I know and live halfway around the world, where I don't know anybody."

"You know me."

"Not really. Not lately. You moved away from me long before you moved to Malaysia. We've been living apart for years. This just makes it official"

She punched off, her sketched face freezing and fading to black.

Ben flung the screen across the room. It slid the length of the apartment and came to rest against the base of the toilet, in the slaughterhouse.

17. Mystic With Spit

This is like a movie, Ben thought. The hero has a setback and the next scene he's in a bar, getting drunk and pouring out his troubles to the bartender. Ben hadn't got drunk in years, but he was beginning to now. He usually avoided alcohol and other drugs entirely. He didn't like the feeling of being out of control, and ethanol aged you and destroyed precious brain cells. But now his life was so out of control that a little ethanol was scarcely noticeable. And it did help insulate against the icy flame of rage and sorrow that burned in his chest like liquid nitrogen. Alone in the bare apartment with his scuffed handheld and deflated mattress he had felt so restless he had had to go out. He had struck off blindly up the street. The late evening heat and traffic made him even more agitated, so he turned into the first air conditioned bar he came to.

Bars had certainly changed, or maybe it was just K.L. This place didn't even call itself a bar. It was one of those link parlors. The patrons, mostly young people, all wore link circlets, like wrap-around shades with thick ear pieces that gripped the temples. Most were tuned into the three piece band on the small stage in the corner. The music seemed screechy and discordant, but most of the young people were nodding and swaying in time with the beat. Some had their links also tuned into each other, their bodies intertwined, fingers tapping on breast and throat in time to the music.

The bill of fare was limited to beer, wine, kef, and brandy. The beer tasted sour and ricey, so after he cooled off, Ben switched to brandy, which tasted more like rum laced with licorice. He stared into the blue tinted mirror behind the bar and saw how old and defeated he looked. He realized he should should never have shown Louise the apartment. He should have called from work, broke it to her gradually. Except she already had her mind made up. She probably decided weeks ago and he was too stupid to figure it out.

He ordered another brandy and stared at his reflection some more. I'm all alone, he thought, imagining himself saying it out loud, trying it on for size. I've got nobody, he continued, "I've got nothing to lose." The bartender glanced at him and he realized he had spoken out loud. Not only that, he thought, I'm talking to myself. Still, it was kind of pleasant, watched himself like a tragic character in a movie, wallowing in a novel depth of misery and self-pity.

Running lines of dialogue in his mind reminded him of his college days, when he often felt he had no fixed personality of his own, but had to try on various characters, feelings, and attitudes to see what fit best.

It was hard to keep his reflection in focus, but his hearing seemed to be improving, because the music was starting to sound better. He turned to watch the musicians. A woman in silver tights, velvet shorts and a tight micropore top slipped onto the stool next to his and smiled.

"Where's your link?" she asked.

Ben shrugged, grinning at her. She was pretty, in an exotic way. Her dark olive skin was set off by metallic gold lip and eye gloss. Her spiky black hair was shaved high above her ears and the skin above her ears was gold plated in a filigree pattern that matched the trim on her custom link circlet. Ben wondered whether the plating improved the link interface, or if it was just decorative. He surprised himself by asking her outright.

"Oh, it's way glossier when you're plated," she said. "You can sync into the groove faster and deeper."

He had not tried the link when it first came out. He had never trusted it, thought it was pop psychology or a fad of progressive politicals, some kind of warmfuzzy group therapy. The first wired ones looked so funny, like old-school Walkmans or jacking into the Matrix. But the new LiteLink circlets were no more than spidery eye glasses worn backwards, run wirelessly off your phone's processor by the biggest selling app ever. They were an offshoot of the direct interface for computers, the brainwave booster that let you control your handheld or headzup mentally.

"Do you use a direct interface on your handheld too?" Ben asked.

"No way. Too much work. That's why God invented fingers." She wiggled her nails in his face, showing off her long nails, plated to match her temples. "But I love the link. DI takes forever to learn, but the link learns you. Here, I'll show you."

She asked the bartender for a house link and leaned closer to Ben, pressing her warm breast against his arm. She licked each temple piece and placed the link over Ben's ears. He smelled licorice on her breath when she said, "It's almost as mystic with spit, but it dries too fast." He felt the wet plastic and her long gold nails on his skull and broke out in goose bumps.

"You gotta link to this band. They're so mystic it's random."

Ben winced as the music started again, amplified by the link set, the bass pumping straight in through his mastoid bone. He didn't know much about link technology. It had something to do with inductive entrainment of brain waves. Kids said it made music and sex better. Some therapists used it to treat mood disorders and epilepsy.

At first he wasn't impressed. It just seemed to emphasize the lower notes of the music, but he felt nothing else.

"I don't get it," he said, shrugging to the girl.

"Wait for the groove," she said, "It takes a minute." She put her hand over his on the bar and tapped her long nails against his wrist.

71

Sure enough, soon the music seemed to change. What was loud and insistent became compelling. When the lead guitarist started to sing, Ben felt his own throat open up as if he was singing too. The music seemed to flow through him like waves of water, warm and silky smooth. He was swaying and tapping his feet and grinning like an idiot at the girl.

"Try this," she said, grinning back. She took her circlet off, touched it to Ben's, and put it back on. The music seemed amplified without getting louder. The drums suddenly seemed more important, more eloquent, imparting subtle secrets that he almost grasped. The girl was tapping out rhythms on his forearm in counterpoint to the music. Ben was amazed at her skill.

"I'm Clarissa," she said when the set was over, "What's your name?"

Ben told her. He told her a little about why he was in K.L. and she seemed fascinated by everything he said. He in turn was charmed by her every word, however trivial and commonplace. Somehow the link made a typical barroom exchange seem profoundly interesting and full of subtle meaning.

They talked and drank and talked some more. Clarissa told him fascinating stories of her adventures traveling with a band from Borneo, dealing in gray market organ futures, and trend spotting for a Lombok couture pirate. After an hour, Ben was seeing double and his link set clattered to the bar top during a fit of laughter. The bartender snatched it away and gave Clarissa a hard look.

"Let's get out of here," she said. "do you have a place?"

"Yeah, sure," Ben said. His tongue felt thick and he had to concentrate very hard on getting off his stool and out the door.

They got lost twice on the way back to his apartment. Clarissa was awfully nice about it. When they stumbled into the lobby of his new building, their way was blocked by a tall blond woman wielding the same automatic pistol the Chinese girl had earlier. The gun didn't surprise Ben this time. It already seemed like a normal part of the décor to Ben and he was proud of how quickly he was adapting to K.L. culture.

"Who do you want?" the blond asked in a heavy Australian accent. Her blond hair was short and almost white. She had shaved and plated temples like Clarissa's.

"I live here," Ben said. "Just moved in today."

She looked at her clipboard. "Name?"

"Ben Rasmussen."

"ID?"

He pulled out his battered handheld and showed her. She peered past the error messages and dead pixels, comparing his ID photo to his grinning face.

"What about her?" she asked Ben, indicating Clarissa.

"Just a friend."

The blond looked at Clarissa and then at Ben. "Old buddies, huh?" she asked, tilting her head and narrowing her eyes again. The she relented and stepped aside.

"Have a nice night." They went upstairs.

18. Diamond in a Dirty Sock

The next morning Ben woke to someone banging on the door. He was half on and half off the half-inflated air mattress. He vaguely remembered an argument about who should blow the mattress up, with some drunken jesting about blow jobs. But he didn't remember anything sexual beyond that, and he still had his clothes on. He must have fallen asleep. Clarissa? Was that her name?

The pounding on the door resumed.

"Just a minute," he yelled, starting a pain in his head that throbbed in time with the knocking. He must be sick, he felt so awful.

He opened the door. It was the blond Australian girl,

looking strong and perky and bright as sunlight. She was wearing a yellow jumpsuit with purple slashes that hurt Ben's eyes. He felt like a million-year-old mummy by contrast.

"What?" he asked.

"This," she answered, holding up his handheld, "is yours, I think."

"How did you get it?"

"Your so-called friend picked it up on her way out last night. Her bag seemed heavier coming down the stairs than going up, so I searched it"

"Thanks," Ben said. He felt a little dizzy and stepped back to catch his balance.

"Are you alright?"

"No. Sick."

"I'm sure. You were warp face last night."

"Excuse me," Ben said. He left the door open, left the girl standing there, and ran to the bathroom to throw up. He brushed his teeth and splashed a lot of cold water into his face.

He remembered the open front door and went to close it. The girl was in the kitchen, brewing chox in his new pot.

"You need a cup of this," she said. "The caffeine will help the headache and the 'dorphins will help the guilt. Some aspirin would be green too—you got any?"

Ben opened his suitcase and rummaged around for an aspirin.

"Jesus," the girl said, "What are you, a dope peddler?"

Ben looked at her and at the plastic bags of brightly colored yellow and orange capsules in his suitcase. "No, I'm a scientist. I do drug research. These are test samples."

She poured two cups, handed him one, and sat cross legged on the floor in one smooth motion. "I'm Glory B. 'B' for Banks."

"Thanks." Ben shook her hand. He sat on the mattress next to the open suitcase. "I'm Ben." He took four aspirin with the steaming hot chox. He was feeling a little better.

"Don't they teach you in science school not to link up

74

with a wanker like that Clarissa?"

"I don't usually link up with anybody. She seemed nice, and the music was so, so..."

"Oh you poor baby, never linked up before, then you link up with a hooker in a bar?"

"I didn't know."

"Never link up with anyone you don't know, and don't link to a band you don't like when you're flat. Girls like that Clarissa will take advantage."

"She seemed so nice. You didn't shoot her, did you?"

"Nah. That piece is so shaggy I'm afraid to pull the trigger."

"Well anyway, thanks for getting my handheld back."

"I'm afraid she broke your 'vice—the case is cracked and it's all over error messages."

"No, it was already broken. I threw it across the room last night."

"How come?"

Ben told her about Louise and the move to K.L. and his transfer to ChemGen. As he told the story for the second time to the second pretty girl in twenty-four hours, he had that feeling of being in a movie again. In scene one the hero's wife divorces him and in scene two he's making it with women half his age. Well, not making it. So far all he'd gotten was a headache and a hot drink. Glory got up and went to refill their cups.

"This is awfully nice of you," he said, "fixing me chox and listening to my story."

"I have this thing I do." She handed him his cup and sat next to him on the mattress. "Every day I try to make a real connection with at least one person I meet. It has to be some kind of contact at a deeper level than hi, how's it going? Or pleased to meet you."

"And today it's me?"

"I guess so." She lifted one of the Rejuven bags out of his suitcase and examined the drugs. "What do these do? Any simulants?"

"No, they don't do a thing to enhance virtual reality. They're supposed to make you younger."

"Go on. Pull the other one."

"No, really. They make mice younger. Monkeys and rats too. They just don't work so well on humans."

"You tried them on yourself?"

"No, they're still experimental. They've only been tried on prison volunteers."

"Volunteers, that's a laugh," Glory shut the suitcase. "I've been in prison myself, back home. You volunteer for what they tell you to volunteer for. Why try to make people live longer anyway? Life's too long as it is."

"You say that because you're young. When you're as old as I am, you'll be very interested in being young again."

"What's so bad about getting old? Old people have all the money and power. You can do anything you want."

"Not really." Ben massaged his temples. "I can't shake off this hangover. I can't run for bus and catch it."

"Big deal. You can afford to take a day off, or take a cab."

"I suppose." Ben felt at a loss to explain to this gorgeous girl how much he hated getting old, how he considered death personally insulting, how he sensed death sometimes lurking behind his eyeballs, waiting for him to blink so it could pull the plug.

"How old are you anyway?" she asked.

"I'm sixty, or will be next Tuesday."

"Happy birthday."

"Not so happy. I'm obsessed with birthdays. Every birthday since I was thirty I've thought 'is my life a third over? half over?'"

"Is that why you research youth drugs?"

"Yeah, I suppose. But I wonder if it's worth it. It's not good enough to keep this sixty year old body chugging along for another hundred years. In the Havana Disneyworld I saw a 1952 Desoto from the Commie era that had been kept running

76

with parts from blacksmith shops and old tractors and Russian limousines. Who wants a body like that? I don't want to just live to be very, very old. I want to feel young for a very, very long time. My drug will also make you feel young."

"What do you mean 'feel young'?"

"I mean the energy, the resilience of youth. I want to fall asleep drunk under a table at four in the morning, jump up at six AM with a cast iron erection, looking for action." He smiled, looking into her eyes. At the mention of erections, his own member stirred. "Well, I don't actually want to live like that again, despite what you see here this morning. But I want the same capacity for non-stop living."

Glory was shaking her head. "It ain't so great to be young. You got plenty of energy, but no traction. No say in anything, no power. Nobody lets you do anything real, so the energy just gets wasted.

"That's an artifact of a ridiculously short lifespan. You're forced to squander the energy of youth cornering money and love and status. Just about the time you're in a position to accomplish something important, you run out of steam. Your muscles and mind turn to mush just when you need them most. It's weird that we've evolved a mind that can grasp eternity, and yet it's trapped in this piss-poor, three-score-and-ten protoplasm like a diamond in a dirty sock."

Did I really say that? Ben asked himself. I must still be drunk. His head drooped and his eyes closed. He was embarrassed about getting so carried away. He was afraid he might cry or throw something again.

Glory moved over and put her arm around him. "It's okay. Everything's green."

"I'm sorry. It just makes me so mad." He put his head on her shoulder. "I think sometimes I get mad just to stay ahead of the emptiness. Anger energizes, keeps your eyes open."

She pulled him closer, "Go down tempo, stop thinking about it for a while."

"I can't stop thinking. I feel I'm wasting time, every

minute I'm not thinking, creating, analyzing, planning how to outwit the darkness. But my batteries are wearing out, my bulbs getting dim. The very problem I'm attacking is attacking me back, and I'm losing."

He reached for her breast and she turned smoothly away, kissed his forehead, and rose effortlessly to her feet.

"You should log off for a while," She said. "You'll feel better. Just sleep, no thinking."

"Okay," Ben crawled over to the mattress and rolled up in the blanket. "Thanks for listening."

"Right, no problem. Glad to help out a new friend."

...and only friends, Ben thought, shutting his eyes. She's too nice to tell me I'm too old for her. What a pathetic old fool I am. He pulled the blanket up over his head and fell into the darkness of a deep and troubled sleep.

19. Protoplasmic Veritas

The following night, Ben sneaked into a ChemGen lab after the second shift technicians left at midnight. Working alone in the dim pool of light from the analyzer interface screen, it took him three tries to set up a simple assay run on the machine. He hadn't run this kind of lab equipment himself for a few years, and the machine was both simpler and more complex than he remembered it. Finally it was chuckling and humming to itself, parsing the long molecular sentence that was RC12.

Ben was testing some of the Kalimer Rejuven doses he had brought with him from the states. Something Glory said about trusting nobody but yourself gave him the idea that the Kalimer quality control department might have skimped on its testing or falsified data. Perhaps the drug that failed the human trials was not the correct formulation. It was unlikely, since it meant that quality control was either incompetent or harboring a saboteur, but it was a place to start, something that he could check here and now.

A muted beep brought him back to the midnight lab and told him that his sample was finally analyzed. He punched up a standard profile display. The peaks and valleys and colors of the profile looked right. He brought out the disk he had stolen from Kalimer and loaded it into a reader. He ported the correct Rejuven profile from his stolen disk to the analysis program and punched "compare." The screen flashed "99.9839% match."

There was nothing wrong with the pills. No contamination, no tampering, no sabotage. Durance, Inc.'s convicts were getting the correct formulation. They should be enjoying a second adolescence, an ironic joke for the lifers, since it meant many extra years of confinement and "voluntary" service to society.

From years of his own research and reading the literature of others' work, Ben knew what to expect in terms of transferable drug effects between rat and human populations. What if the disappointing results were just a lie? Science was always about trust, rather than truth. Scientists had always trusted each other to report the data accurately and completely, without spin, without slanting or shaving a point or simplifying by omission to support their hypotheses. But science was more and more at the mercy of politicians, of profiteers and marketeers who were neither in the trust business nor overly concerned with truth.

Assume for a moment that the drug was working on the human subjects, but Data Analysis was watering down the results, faking data to make the drug look like a washout. Was it possible that the human trials were going according to plan, and the plan included cheating Ben Rasmussen out of credit? Could it be that they got him out of the way in Malaysia so that they could finish testing and market Rejuven without him? Were they cheating him out of credit for the drug that was his last chance for financial security? Kalimer was certainly capable of lies and half truths. He'd learned that much at ChemGen. They seemed to be maneuvering to produce Rejuven, or something very much like it, in large quantities.

And what about all the acquisitions and mergers in the last year? Corporate mergers and alliances with major suppliers and subcontractors were a common first step in announcing a major new drug.

Or was he kidding himself? Was he too proud to admit that he had failed with Rejuven? Was he crazy to believe in himself? Was he so greedy for the patent bonuses, so desperate to wipe out his corporate debt load that he would imagine a conspiracy against himself rather than admit failure? Maybe he was just washed up, well past his creative and intellectual peak, sliding into mediocrity and oblivion. Louise and Kapoor and others certainly had testified to that.

Ben opened the bottle of Rejuven and took out one of the large capsules. There was a way to answer these questions, a way to know for sure, at the gut level, as it were. He could take the drug himself. He could break the rules he had respected all his professional life, and experiment on himself. It would be stupid, and a violation of all the principles of experimental science. The investigator must remain objective, separate and aloof from the subjects. That's what prisoners were for. If he took the drug and they found out, that fact alone could get him fired.

He thought of Jonas Salk, back in the twentieth century, administering his unproven polio vaccine to himself and his wife and kids. What if he had erred and the poliovirus he injected was not completely dead? What if there had been unforeseen side effects? Salk had lucked out, he and his family came up with robust polio antibodies and no adverse side effects, just as predicted.

Salk did his work before the patent bonus system was in place. In fact, he never even patented his vaccine, effectively giving it away to the world. Ben had always wondered if that gesture was, at least in part, motivated by guilt over the risks he had taken by experimenting on himself and his family?

Salk aside, Ben had to know, in his own flesh, what it

felt like. Statistics weren't enough anymore, weren't to be trusted. Statistics could be falsified and manipulated. he needed the truth of the flesh, the protoplasmic veritas, the bodily data that comes moment by moment bubbling up from the cellular level, the meat meaning, straight from his own corpus, unmediated by the system that he increasingly mistrusted.

What did he have to lose? Either Rejuven would work or it wouldn't. If it worked, he would feel young again, regain his creative spark, his energy and drive. He'd become walking, breathing, irrefutable proof that the drug worked. He could kick start his stalled brain and figure out how to seize control of the situation, make Kalimer reinstate him and give credit where it was due.

He wouldn't know for a while. He'd have to take the capsules for several weeks to build up to the optimum level of effectiveness. But some results should show up soon.

And if it didn't work, what then? What if he had some of the serious side effects? Seizures? Well, if it didn't work, at least he'd know where he stood. Knowing you're a failure couldn't be much worse than constantly suspecting it. Maybe the side effects would be fatal. So be it. If Rejuven was that bad, if his failure was that massive, he'd have no reason to live anyway.

Ben tossed the capsule into the back of his throat and swallowed it dry in a horrid, scratchy gulp.

20. Ellipses of Desire

Ben trotted down the stairs to the lobby with a spring in his step. After just three weeks on Rejuven, his knees were free of pain and his legs seemed stronger. It was early for any significant synovial deposition to have taken place, so maybe it was just the anti-inflammatory effect. Whatever, he didn't care. Maybe he'd drop into a Body Beautiful on the way home and have an X-ray, or what did they call it? *Melihat ke dalam*: a peek inside.

"Hi Ben," Glory's daughter Lilly said, starting up the stairs in the other direction.

"Hold up, sport," Ben said, "I've got something for you." He handed her a key.

"What's this?"

"Your own key. You can let yourself in. Just lock the apartment when you leave."

"I'll give the key back tonight."

"Nah, keep it. I trust you."

She grinned and bounded up the stairs. Lilly had been spending more and more time in Ben's air-conditioned apartment, a much better place to do her schoolwork than in the stuffy lobby with her mom.

Glory was just sitting down in the lobby with her 'vice and gun.

"Thanks, Ben. That was nice."

"She's a good kid. Very mature for eleven."

"I really appreciate you letting her spend time in your apartment. Our tent is so hot, even when you wet it down, and then Jenkins complains about wasting water."

"You're welcome."

"I'd keep her here with me in the lobby but it's still hot, and Jenkins complains, says it lowers the tone of the building, it's a lobby, not a daycare."

"Jenkins, that wanker. He should eat shit and die for wanting a little girl to swelter in a tent to preserve his tone. Say, I noticed your coconut milk is almost gone in the fridge. Want me to pick some up on the way home?"

"That would be glossy."

"I'll pick up some chicken too. You guys want to help me cook dinner? We could make some ayam percik."

"Sounds good."

"Okay, see you later." He sauntered out the gate and down to the cab stand. A tri-shaw was just pulling up, powered by a young woman, brown and short with long stringy muscles in her bare legs, knotted like tree roots. Ben gave her ChemGen's address and jumped into the bouncy seat. As they pounded up the street, he watched her buttocks pumping before him and felt a stirring in his groin.

Lately he'd been noticing all the young women in their brightly colored skirts and shorts, all the delectable young things dressed for the hot climate and relaxed secular expectations of what a woman was allowed to wear. Or the older ones in sarongs or saris, swaying like palms, the impression of a hip or a breast appearing and fading away in a fascinating rhythm. He was horny all the time.

Yesterday he had taken a lunch break and gone for a walk to burn off some of his restless energy. He found himself following two shapely Malaysian admin caste girls through a crowded street market, drawn by a magnetic attraction he hadn't felt since he was in his twenties, orbiting young women like a captured asteroid, helplessly tracing the ellipses of desire. He had to tear himself away and return to work. Once there, he couldn't concentrate on the job until he had ducked into the men's room to masturbate. A few quick strokes was all it took these days.

It was quite a change from the last few years with Louise, when sex was a semi-monthly ritual that required strategic planning and negotiation. Too often their lovemaking was performed in the shadow of their childlessness, bringing up memories of their daughter Janey, dead forever at age two of MEI, Multiple Environmental Insult. She was basically allergic to the whole world, her immune system a firestorm of reactions that just tore her apart.

They talked from time to time about having another child, about implants and surrogates and such, but they never got around to it. The time never seemed right again. They both dove into work, lost the habit of romance, became disconnected from friends with kids. Louise's hydrological model of the watershed became more important that the architecture of marriage. Foundations crumbled. For years they had been more like roommates than lovers or spouses. No wonder she didn't join him in K.L. There was nothing here for her.

Funny, Janey would have been ten by now, almost the same age as Glory's daughter Lilly. She never would have been as robust and spunky as Lilly. He could imagine them playing together, Lilly and Janey, the Australian tent girl and the sickly American. Kind of like Glory and himself, an odd couple.

21. Delicious Power

"You can't do it that way," C. F. Chow said, her jowls quivering, "It's stupid."

"Now Charity," Ben said, addressing her by her hated first name, "you haven't really thought this through." He pointed to the flow chart on the lab bench in front of them. "Once I've reprogrammed the splicer and put in another centrifuge, this bottleneck goes away. The improvement to the workflow alone will raise production, even without the new processes."

In his first couple of weeks at ChemGen Ben was scared of C. F. Chow. She was an intimidating package, with her dogged enthusiasm for the creepy Body Beautiful harvest operations, her contempt for weakness and sentiment, her ironclad opinions, her rapid fire Cantonese diatribes. Then he learned that C. F. Chow stood for Charity Forbearance Chow, and that delighted him. She was so not her name, not a bit charitable and never inclined to forbear anyone or anything that annoyed her. Now he didn't fear her. He just hated her. But it was a cheerful hatred. Kind of invigorating.

She pointed to another part of the chart. "Sixteen deciliters per hour? You will never do so much."

"I think I will. Your old protocol was okay, but slow and inefficient. You'd refine and purify at one step, then introduce more carriers and contaminants down the line and have to refine and purify all over again."

"So you say. But all changes are not necessary. You make more than we need for labeling law."

"That's right, and you'll be glad to have them a year from now, when Kalimer and other firms are in the market for lab cells." His plan was to crank out more synthetic biological materials and reduce the need for harvested fractions. It was an interesting problem and had got his creative juices flowing. He could see ways to get the percentage of synthetics up to fifty percent or more in a few months, without spending much more than the current budget for the Synth Lab.

"This must go to budget committee," Chow said.

"Fine, you let me know how that meeting comes out. Just don't expect me to attend it."

"You need to explain to committee."

"No, I don't. They won't understand it anyway."

"I don't understand already. Why you won't come to meeting?"

"Let me tell you, Charity. In my experience, committee meetings always have the same agenda." He counted off on his fingers, "Item one: infighting and political maneuvering. Item two: rampant self-interest and frantic ass-covering. Item three: manipulation, lies, and outright stupidity. And through it all, the scent of bullshit in the air so thick you could cut it with a letter opener."

Her eyes got almost round, then she blinked three times, having a hard time processing this outburst. Nobody spoke to their nominal superior this way, not at Kalimer, and not even at a less prestigious outfit like ChemGen. He was sending up the chain of command the kind of diatribe that normally was only sent down the chain. It was breaking the rules, like making water run uphill or running an electrical current backwards through a diode.

Chow took a breath and seemed to gather herself, perhaps about to launch her own diatribe and send the water flowing back downhill again. Ben stopped her by draping his arm over her bony shoulders.

"You see Charity, doing science by committee is like phone sex, a pale imitation of the real thing."

She squirmed out from under him.

"It's a miracle that anything ever gets discovered," Ben continued, "much less brought to market. If you want me to re-vamp the Synth Lab, this is how it has to be done. You and the budget committee will just have to trust me." He gave her a big sunny grin.

Chow shook her head again and turned away. She scur-ried out of the lab and slammed the door.

Ben laughed and turned back to his flow chart. Dog Chow would stew over his outburst and his inappropriate touch-ing, but she wouldn't do anything about it. She was too afraid that he was a Kalimer spy, and it gave him delicious power. It was great fun, saying what you actually thought for a change.

His nose was sore. He rubbed it and tried to remember how long it had been since he had a pimple. He took it as a good sign that the Rejuven was working, inducing a kind of artificial adolescence.

He chuckled out loud again and beat a paradiddle on the stainless steel fume hood above his head. The look of dismay on Chow's doggy face was delectable. He had been ducking committee meetings lately, and getting away with it. He was us-ing the ChemGen anxiety over the merger with Kalimer to his advantage, getting his way without the usual machinations. Or maybe this was how the machinations worked at a higher lev-el. He especially enjoyed using such noncorporate words like "trust."

22. Glorious

Ben caught a cab for home, and noticed that he thought of his apartment as home. Home was no longer the house in Santa

Rosa with Louise, or the Mono Lake house. He didn't even miss his plane or his routine at the Kalimer gym. Home was the Malay Express: four shabby rooms in a row like a train; the rusty front gate with the razor wire; Glory B or Chinese Dotty guarding the lobby; Lilly Banks bouncing up and down the stairs; Superintendentman Jenkins grousing about people acting common in the common areas.

It was amazing how fast you could adapt and settle in to a new life. He felt like a different person already, more of a regular citizen, with more in common with what he used to call privately the "little people," the masses. He used to not see them at all, not appreciate the fact that they are just as real as he was. Everybody¬¬–the tri-shaw driver, the barkeep, the blind woman in her virch goggles selling mangoes on the median strip—they each were just as real as Ben Rasmussen. They each had a universe inside them. They each were the entire universe from their point of view They each starred in the longest running miniseries ever—their own.

He directed the cabby to Mr. Tam's little market and bookie joint, near home. He picked up some milk, some rolls and butter, some star fruit, a rooty vegetable thing, and a package of noodles. He couldn't lose. His choices would either inspire Glory to introduce him to a new dish, or provide a good laugh, and they'd have noodles again.

At home, Glory and Lilly both had screens going. Lilly was watching one of her boy band videos, her screen blossoming with explosions and lightning flashes, the shrill, insistent sambabong music leaking past her link speakers like a mosquito's whine. Ben tapped her on the top of her head to get her attention.

"Hi," he said, "What you got there?"

"Heros Four from Japan. On their Apocalypso tour." Her head was rocking back forth to the beat, a timeless teenage metronome.

"Reminds me of the Fab Four."

"The what?"

87

"Never mind." He set his string bag with the groceries on the tiny kitchen counter where Glory's handheld was propped up against the chox maker. She was watching some kind of talk show where people were going on about grammar school linking. A woman in a social services vest was counting off points on her fingers, her hands shaking with passion: "When school kids link they get over-stimulated emotionally. They feed on each other's anger and fear and depression. They get ideas about sex that they're too young to handle. Linking at that age is like a gateway drug to teen pregnancy."

Glory turned the handheld off.

"That woman's a dimwit," she said. She opened Ben's bag and started unloading the groceries.

"What about you?" Ben asked, "Do you know the Fab Four?"

"Of course," Glory said, "The Beatles, right?"

"Very good."

"Paul McCarney, John Lennox, George...somebody, and..." She looked up, frowned.

"Go on, one more."

"Frank Sinatra?"

"Close enough."

"What's this?" Glory asked, freeing the root vegetable from the string bag. "Are you trying to tell me something, matey?"

"I have no idea what that is, but it looked like you, so I bought it." The root was twisted and ugly, forked like two legs, with gnarled bumps that could have been arms.

"It looks more like you." She threw the empty string bag at him. "This is what Lumpy mamas brew up for their husbands when things are getting boring in the sack."

Ben felt a flush rise up his neck. He had been blushing like a schoolboy lately, suddenly hot and sweaty for no reason. He made himself laugh it off.

"Save it for your boyfriend."

"Yeah, I wish. You're a terror in the store. You'll buy

anything." She put the root on the windowsill above the sink. "Pasta okay for dinner?"

She set about filling a pot with water, pulling ingredients from the fridge, creating an agreeable clatter. Ben liked how she pronounced "pasta" like a Brit, with a flat a sound.

Lilly turned off her 'vice called to Ben, "We have a game of Monarchy to finish."

"Okay." He sat on the floor across the board from her.

"If I was you," Lilly said, "I'd watch out for my Queenie."

Ben studied the board. His pieces were in trouble. He didn't have to let Lilly win. At eleven she was as wily at Monarchy as Eleanor of Aquitaine. It was all he could do to keep up. Already his King had been deposed twice and decapitated once. Actually, it would be nice if she'd let him win once in a while.

"Take that," he said, moving one of his Ministers into her Sphere of Influence.

"Not so fast, Mr. American cowboy." She enfiladed with a Terrorist and a Lobbyist, and his Minister was history.

"Free roll, free roll!" she said, grabbing the large and small dice.

"Crikey," Ben said, seeing another decapitation in the offing. "If we were playing regular chess, this would never happen to a nice guy like me."

"Chess is boring. The board is dumb cardboard, it just sits there."

"Yeah, you're right. This is better." The Monarchy smart board changed its graphics as the game progressed, colors and shapes shifting with the balance of power. He had to admit it was pretty glossy.

He moved a General up two spaces, hoping to set up a coup d'état, and tried to distract her from the game: "So Lilly, what in your opinion is the best boy band ever? Heros Four?"

"They're good, but not the best. It's hard to say because it depends. For sambabong, maybe Heros, but what about Wireheads? For Vim the best is Glossy Posse, everybody knows that.

But if you're talking wordpop, it's a tossup between Maul Rats and Fracklash." She neutralized his General with a Spy and played a traitor card.

"There you go," she said, "Sorry. Beheaded again."

Ben sighed.

They ate the noodles with butter and garlic and leftover soy strips, all washed down by a decent local beer. Ben got them laughing with his imitation of Dog Chow.

Glory said, "Explain something to me. Say they start selling this drug to everybody, and it makes everybody live longer."

"Okay."

"Doesn't that make all the overpopulation and pollution and food shortages worse?"

"Maybe if it happened all at once, everywhere. But it won't be like that. Changes come slowly, life expectancy would creep up, and people will have time to adapt."

"It doesn't make sense to me. It seems like trying to make life longer for some people is going to make life worse for most people."

"That's just how it looks on the surface. It's a paradox. If some people live longer, they'll live different lives. They'll have more time to solve things like resource allocation, carbon imbalances, all kinds of inequalities."

"Well, people live pretty long right now, and I don't see them solving my problems. We still live in a tent and Lilly's two grades behind kids back home. It still takes three salaries to support two people."

"I guess I don't have an answer for that, at least not in the short term. I'm a scientist, and I do my best to solve the problems in my science. That's my job. I have to trust that the crop scientists and the weather guys and other scientists in other fields will do their jobs too. And somehow we'll muddle through."

"That's the goal, the big plan for all this technology and shit? Muddle through?"

Ben grinned at her. "Right, like the Buddha says, you got to follow the Muddle path."

"You're horrible." She handed him the rest of her beer to finish. "I have another question."

"Shoot."

"How do you personally fit into all this? Experimenting on yourself? Isn't that illegal or unethical or something? Won't you get into trouble?"

Ben wet the rim of his wine glass and stroked it with his finger, creating an eerie soundtrack for his response. "Well, it's complicated. If Rejuven works out, I could be famous. There's lots of famous drug researchers who experimented on themselves."

"Yeah, like who?"

Jonas Salk. He took the polio vaccine to prove it worked. Gave it to his whole family, too. And Albert Hoffman, the guy who discovered LSD. He was a notorious acid tripper."

"Maybe they'll make a movie about you."

"Yeah, one of those inspirational biopics."

"No, I was thinking horror, like The Fly. Or Radioacticon. Or Dr. Jeckyl and Mr. Hyde."

Ben contorted his face, trying to transform into a monstrous Mr. Hyde.

"Stop, please," Glory said. "You look like you're going to barf."

After dinner Lilly fell asleep on the couch. Glory made tea, grating some of the root Ben bought into the cups.

"It actually makes pretty good tea," she said. "That aphrodisiac stuff is just folklore." She turned off the lights in the living room and kitchen, and they retreated to the bedroom so as not to wake Lilly.

They drank their tea sitting on the bed.

"This is nice," Glory said. "Peaceful. Cozy. Safe."

"Why don't you play us some music?"

She nodded and pulled her handheld out of her bag. She also pulled out a pair of link headsets.

"This okay with you?" she asked, holding up the links. "It will make the music better."

"Love to." Ben felt like he was suddenly short of breath.

She reached toward him and draped the link around the back of his head, ruffling his hair. He could smell garlic and something flowery and a hint of the day's sweat on her skin. She donned her link and started the music. It was something droney and vaguely Indian.

As he listened and sipped his tea, Ben felt the music seep into his body, each muscle fiber vibrating ever so slightly to the overtones of the stringed instruments. Glory looked at him over the rim of her cup, and her eyes seemed to glow. Her whole face was suffused with light and he thought that he had never known anyone who so perfectly fitted her name. She was Glorious.

The harsh lights in the shabby room began to seem radiant and the room itself took on a glimmer and glow, like they were on stage in some fabulous play, heroic figures center stage in the spotlight. The music was a pit orchestra playing for them alone.

They moved closer together, gliding as one. She kissed him, then he kissed her. Their clothes seemed to melt away and they came together. Ben was astonished at how close he felt to Glory, how perfectly they fit and moved together, how steel hard he had become, and how quickly he came.

"Sorry," he said. "It caught me by surprise."

"That's okay. My turn next time."

They cuddled for a while, and then there was a next time, and they came at the same glorious instant. Ben was astonished and grateful. It had been a long time. It had been years since he had been so passionately absorbed in sex, since he could count absolutely on his equipment, since he could do it twice in one night, much less in one hour. He was so grateful he felt tears pinching his eyes closed.

"See, you're not so old as you think," Glory said

"Nice of you to say."

"I'm not just being nice. You really do look a little younger these days. You could pass for fifty, maybe even late forties, if you dyed your hair."

"Right now, I don't care how long I live, if I could just live this moment over and over."

"You'd get bored of it."

"Never."

She shifted position and retrieved her cup from the floor. "Seems like this is the real immortality. Making love, making babies." She smiled at his sudden look of alarm. "Don't' worry, Ben. I'm on the implant. You can't make a baby in me. Even if you did, I could always stop by Body Beautiful and take care of it."

"Don't say that. Those places creep me out."

"They're necessary. What's a girl to do, otherwise? They can't be having babies all the time. Better to just have the ones you can take care of, and let the rest go."

"I know, but with all the birth control options these days, it's simple to take precautions."

"Like you just did?"

"Touché."

"Anyway, I don't think they do that many borts. It's the Botox and the plastic surgery that's the big business, all the lid jobs and chin jobs so that the slants can look all BESM–Big Eyes, Small Mouth."

"Still, it creeps me out."

"Beauty parlors always creep guys out, even when they just did hair and nails. What creeps me out are those M&Ms."

"Candy?"

"No, those migratory melanin tattoos. They end up looking like wart farms in ten years. Then you have to get them lasered off, and the skin is never quite the same again." She rubbed a scaly patch on her upper arm.

"Oh, poor baby." He kissed the spot.

Glory collected Lilly from the couch and carried her out to their tent. She didn't want to stay the night and then have to explain things to her daughter.

"We've had enough new business tonight," she said, going out the door. "I'll catch up with you tomorrow."

Ben sat at the kitchen table after they left, massaging his temples. He had a headache, and another pimple was forming on his chin. But he felt good. In fact, he felt amazing and amazed.

He logged onto the California Superior Court website and found Louise's divorce filing. He stared at it without reading it for what seemed like a minute, then he noticed the time stamp–he'd been sitting there twenty minutes, thinking nothing, seeing nothing. He wondered if this is what it feels like to have a petit mal seizure?

He clicked the "Agree to file" box and pressed his thumb to the bimetrix oval on the screen. After the mandatory ten-day waiting period, they would no longer be man and wife. Their property might take months to split up and turn back to Kalimer and the banks, but their union was easily disposed of.

He felt like a different person. A younger person, but not a younger Ben Rasmussen. He felt like a younger someone else. He felt like going to confession, telling someone about everything he had ever done that he regretted. He needed to be forgiven for so much. For indenturing himself so thoroughly to Kalimer, for trifling with his prison subjects by making them feel younger and more aggressive and then getting them into trouble. For destroying Louise's life. She'd have to get a better job if she wanted to hang onto the house, and she was too old to get much of a job.

He let the 'vice slip from his fingers and placed his head on his hands, falling asleep right there at the kitchen table. An hour later he woke and shuffled into the bedroom, fell into bed and went back to sleep, thinking he really should get up and brush his teeth and turn off the lights.

23. Clock Running Backwards

At work Ben kept a secret lab notebook hidden inside the access panel of the replicator. He took it out whenever he noticed a new reaction to the Rejuven, or had some other thought to record. At first his notes were brief and succinct. As time went on, he elaborated and extended his comments, rambling further and further afield. The lab notebook became his diary, his confidant, and his friend in a friendless job. He started the notebook at first to foil anyone who might try to hack his computer notes, but he continued because it was more satisfying that the traditional digital record.

The usual lab log was a carefully edited resumé for the research team members, showing how brilliant they were, performing flawlessly at each step on the way to their groundbreaking discovery. Ben came to appreciate the enforced candidness of an analog notebook, written indelibly in ink on dead tree paper, preserving every false lead, every red herring, every erroneous interpretation. His Rejuven notebook told it like it was:

Day 3: Feel hot, flushed. 37.2 fever. Vivid dreams last night.

Day 8: Night sweats. Dreaming about my mother and Louise, all mixed up. Ruminating during the day about Glory. Kind of depressed and excited at the same time. Stronger emotional highs and lows. Dreaming my day away.

Day 9: Blood pressure slightly higher, 135/85. Have to watch that. Facial wrinkles filling in, lips seem fuller with more collagen. Skin feels tighter, smoother.

Day 12: Arm muscles noticeably larger and stronger—biceps, forearms. It seems like it is easier to achieve a muscle training effect with ordinary exertion. I could pump iron and get really buffed-out. More energy, can walk a little farther, faster, longer.

Day 13: More night sweats. Forgot to take blood pressure three days in a row. I'm relying more on my feelings of the moment to power me through different situations, rather than planning or problem solving. Taking a more intuitive approach. Or am I becoming a moody teenager again? Sometimes my thinking is clear as glass, sometimes I don't think at all and just space out.

Day 15: Teased Chow again, got yelled at. What a tiresome woman. She wants me to do things that are just too boring and pointless. Life is too short to live by her rules. There is so much to do. My research has barely scratched the surface. I need an extra hundred years for starters. I'm living too early—if I was only born a hundred years later, I might live forever. I feel like I will miss that train. No, that's the wrong metaphor. I feel like I have almost achieved escape velocity, but not quite. I'll never break free. The black hole will suck me down and I'll disappear into the event horizon, while those born just a century after me will have the velocity to break free and go to the stars.

Day 18: Death is scary, mysterious, maddening. It seems such an affront, so inconceivable. To lose consciousness in a way that means not waking up in the morning, not rebooting the brain and body, but game over forever. My meat brain just can't imagine that, so I must fight it and defeat it. I must keep charging at the windmill, keep getting knocked on my ass.

Day 19: I am also afraid of life, of day-to-day living, one minute piled on another, undifferentiated time flowing along, being wasted, or wasting me, indifferent, inexorable. Life is just death metered out a spoonful at a time, piling up a mountain of salt to smother and hide me forever. I long to break free, fly, soar above it all, beyond and outside of time and death.

Day 20: Spent 20 minutes staring at myself in a mirror. I no longer look 60. More like a well-preserved 50. Maybe even a dissipated 40, from the right angle, in the right light. My face is the face of a clock running backwards. I've always thought of time as a slow fire, burning my life up a day at a time. Every morning I'd throw another log on the fire and every evening I lie down in the ashes and wonder if I will get up next day. Now I rise like a phoenix every morning, new life from the ashes.

Day 22: When I was a kid, I confused death and the devil, conflating them together as a hooded figure in black with a scythe, red and scaly under the cloak, with forked tail and horns. I think that's right, that's the connection—death is the ultimate evil. It's why murder is the big crime, why vending machine abortions and drone executions bother me so much.

24. Donned and Onned

Glory was peering into her handheld, muttering and cursing.

"What's the matter?" Ben asked.

"Nothing really. I'm just trying to read what Lilly's seeing, but she's too fast. See if you can make it out." She handed him the 'vice.

On the screen he saw a jerky live action video feed. The camera was panning over a display of statuettes in a glass case, each statuette with a printed label.

"What is this?" he asked.

"Lilly's link feed. She's on a school field trip to some museum. She's not looking at the labels long enough for me to read them."

Ben started reading out loud the label that Lilly was looking at: "During the Islamic Revival, 1970-2030, the bomoh shamans were suppressed due to their association with black magic. Today however…"

"Wow," Glory said, "How can you read so fast? You sound like a news anchor."

"Just natural talent, I guess." Ben finished reading the label, getting almost all of it before Lilly turned her head and the link camera away.

"Just like TV," Glory said again.

He felt a little sorry for Glory and other people her age who were functional illiterates compared to folks of his generation. It was why she named her daughter Lilly instead of Lily, a misspelling almost no one noticed or cared about these days. The printed word was dying out thanks to the computer icons, ad logos, and photo menus that made reading less and less necessary to a consumer. A new user-friendly mediagraphics had arisen, with many evolved, intuitive symbols for meaning functions. When people absolutely had to type actual words, they relied on context-savvy software to fix their spelling and grammar, to suggest vocabulary.

"Why are you watching Lilly's field trip?"

"Just making sure she's safe. When one of us goes out, Lilly and I set our links to video/on, slaved to our phones, to keep track of each other. I can see what she's seeing, she can see what I'm seeing. It's a way to know that we are both safe. Look: they're leaving now."

The screen showed the backs of several kids heads as they emerged into the street.

"They'll get on the bus now and she'll be home in about an hour."

"Doesn't she object to losing her privacy?"

She laughed. "Sometimes. When she was little, I made her turn the camera on any time she went out. But I'd turn mine off whenever I didn't want her to see what I was doing or hear what I was saying about her. It didn't take her long to point out that that was not fair. Now we have an agreement: no audio, and we can turn off the cameras for privacy, no questions asked. It took a couple of big fights before we settled that one. She threatened to video poop coming out her ass and upload it to the cloud."

"I'm amazed that she would do this—remember to put on the link set and turn it on."

"Her link is always on her head, haven't you noticed? That's the default for kids her age, links donned and onned. That's why she has such a glazed look in the eyes all the time: she's either listening to one of her boy bands or video chatting with her friends, or both."

"Doesn't that bother you? Her linking with all those kids."

"Not at all. It's a way of finding out who your people are. If you link with someone over and over, you really get to know them. It becomes almost impossible to lie to them, so you stay true or break up."

"It almost sounds like sex for tweenies."

"It's more important than sex. A girl might marry a boy she never slept with, but she shouldn't even go out with a boy who isn't willing to link on the first date. That's the real compatibility."

"I had no idea. I thought Lilly wore hers all the time as a fashion thing."

"Lilly would have her link surgically implanted if she could."

"When I was her age, we felt the same way about our iPods."

"iWhats?"

"Never mind. It dates me."

"No, I'm interested. Not in the 'vice, in you. What were you like when you were Lilly's age, or my age?"

"Hunky as hell." He gave her hip a bump with his own.

"No, what were you like for real? Did you ever really have the fizz you're trying to get back?"

"What do you mean?"

"Some people are just born old and wise. I think maybe that's you."

"I'm a natural born old guy? Thanks a lot."

"No, that's not what I'm saying. I mean that the youth you remember, the hot fizzy kind, that's bullshit. I don't feel hot and fizzy all the time."

"You could fool me." He nuzzled her neck.

"Being young isn't as good as it looks."

"If you're saying I should act my age, I'd rather act your age."

"I think I'm saying you only can be the age you are, at the moment."

"At the moment, I'm not sure what age I am. The calendar says sixty, the mirror says maybe forty-five."

"Forty nine, I'd give you that."

"Thanks." He drew his link out of his pocket and put it on.

"But my heart says I'm eleven, and I want to find out if you're my true friend."

She laughed and put on her link too.

"Okay friend, put on some music and I'll make sure my video feed to Lilly is off. We've got a good fifty minutes before she gets home."

Ben liked hearing her say "home," referring to his apartment. He liked retiring to the bedroom even more. Sex with Glory, linked together, with music playing, was transcendent, timeless, the best ever.

Afterwards he had a headache, pounding with each beat of his heart. His hands were trembling a little, too.

"I'm worried about your headaches," Glory said. "You always get one after we link up."

"It's nothing. It's worth it."

"Even so, are you sure you should be taking that Rejuven? You shouldn't have a headache afterwards."

"It's important for me to know the side effects, to really

experience them and understand them, from the inside out." He clasped his hands together so she wouldn't see them shaking.

"I'm just worried, is all."

"I know, and I appreciate it. But I can handle it. I'm like the guy who looked for the fountain of youth all his life—big risk, big reward."

That night Glory slept in Ben's bed and Lilly slept on the couch. Ben lay awake while they slept, thinking about the fountain of youth. He secretly wanted to be the guy who discovered the fountain of youth and led the world to it. People already lived routinely past 110. If he could push that out to 130 or 140, he might live long enough to see the singularity, the event horizon beyond which mankind falls forever away from death, into the long future, into the stars.

People always worried about what would happen to the earth if humans lived forever. They'd overrun the place and die off from mass starvation or spiraling climatic excursions. Not so, Ben thought. With immortal life in the equation, everything changes. It gives us time to devote to really long term projects, like going to the stars by teleportation or faster than light drive. Birthrates might drop precipitously when we don't need to reproduce new humans just to replace the dead. It's a brand new evolutionary plateau, one that no other species on the planet has reached yet, so who knows how the system will change when we reach that stage?

Another way to view immortality is that it is the end of evolution. With generations living almost forever and a very slow birth rate, there will be almost no evolutionary progress. Or perhaps we'll take over the engine of evolution ourselves, changing our existing bodies in the current generation with technical interventions, adapting right now to cope with changes in the environment, instead of relying on random mutation worked out through many generations.

When it got down to it, Ben didn't really care about what happened in the future. He just wanted to be there to see it happen.

25. Don't Want to Run Out

The InMates TV show gave Ben a window into Kalimer, or maybe a distorted funhouse mirror. Sometimes he thought it was Kapoor's way of sending him messages. In last week's episode, Haunch tried to join the Rejuven human trial and was put on the waiting list. But she couldn't wait. She stole Boob's supply of the new Rejuven capsules, took a handful, and was caught with the rest by the guards doing a cell search.

This week Li'l Piece and Glitz, the twenty-something eye candy of the show, the slutty darlings of the cell block, were folding laundry and rehashing events.

"They put Haunch in solitary again," Li'l Piece said. "Thirty days."

"Serves her right. Bitch took another girl's dose.

"Didn't she know that's stupid? That Rejuven is made up for like one person at a time. Different formula for different people."

"I know," Glitz said. "I heard Boobs was three days without her Rejuven and she sagged an inch." She held her hands cupped before her and demonstrated the subsidence of the famous bosom.

"Yeah, you don't want to run out of that stuff."

26. Pick Any Two Out of Three

"Hello, Dr. Rasmussen." It was Trujib Kapoor, calling from Kalimer in San Francisco. It was fifteen hours earlier there, so he must have got up early to talk live, instead of leaving a message.

"Hello Dr. Kapoor." Ben switched his phone to record the call, using an illegal app that did not throw a flashing red dot into the lower right corner of Kapoor's screen. Kapoor peered up out of the screen, maybe wondering at Ben's changed appearance. Ben hoped he would interpret his newly younger, acned face to be coming through a buggy grooming filter. Finally Kapoor spoke.

"It has come to my attention that you ordered a substantial supply of Rejuven before you left Kalimer, and it has not turned up here at the office. I must ask that you return it without delay."

No pleasantries, no small talk. Ben felt a shiver up his spine. "Really, I don't recall any Rejuven."

Kapoor held up a sheet of paper, "I have your requisition right here. Those capsules are the property of Kalimer and you are not authorized to have them in your possession."

"Oh, that Rejuven. I remember now. I did have some, but I destroyed it."

"Destroyed it?"

"Yes. Burned it up." Metabolically speaking, Ben thought. He smiled.

"This is very serious, Dr. Rasmussen."

"Oh, lighten up, Trudge. What's the big deal? Are you afraid I sold them on the black market for pocket change? Is that going to cut into your millions? You've already cut me out of the Rejuven bonuses. Did that give you a thrill, stealing my ideas, using me for all those years, then tossing me aside when it looked like I might cash out?"

Kapoor look astonished, for him—his eyebrows rose about a millimeter and his forehead took on the slightest suggestions of a wale, if not a wrinkle.

Ben continued, "Or are you afraid I took those Rejuvens? Experimented on myself? Lost my precious objectivity? Went rogue?"

"This is no joking matter. If you give those drugs to someone, or take them yourself, you are in violation of any

103

number of laws. It could have serious repercussions."

"Don't talk to me about repercussions. I know things. I know things you don't want anybody else to know."

"For instance?"

"Rejuven has some serious side effects that you're not reporting. You're transferring prisoners out of the human trials right and left because they're freaking out, emotionally labile and violent. The stem cell sourcing and labeling is from Grimm's Fairytales. The whole charade is run more by the director of the InMates show than by poor Cynthia Lim, your so-called director of research. Whom I know you're fucking on the side, by the way."

"Those are serious allegations." Kapoor moved an inch closer to the camera and squinted his eyes ever so slightly. He called the allegations "serious," not "ridiculous." Interesting.

"I have proof."

"What proof?"

"I guess you'll never know. I've got to go. I'm late for a meeting." He hung up. It was delicious to shake up that stuffed vest and then hang up on him. It made Ben wish he really did have proof and not just suspicions.

Ben really did have a meeting to attend. After putting it off as long as possible, he had to present his lab budget for approval to the finance committee. They met face-to-face, in a real conference room. No virtuality for something as important as money, as risky as spending it, as satisfying as withholding it from someone like Ben who really deserved it. When he walked in late, everyone turned to face him: six bland Asian faces, giving nothing away.

"Sorry I'm late," he said, taking the vacant chair at the foot of the table. "I was chatting with Dr. Kapoor at Kalimer."

Nobody looked particularly impressed. Ben had been at ChemGen for quite a while now, and nobody had been fired or demoted or rolled up or squeezed down—at least not in any way attributable to Ben's presence in the firm. Their fear of him had declined to where it was not very useful in getting his way. Too bad. It was nice while it lasted. He had become accustomed to throwing his weight around, saying what he thought and making people take it.

The chairperson gestured to Ben's budget figures on the overhead screen and said, "We have reviewed your proposed budget, and have some considerable reservations about it," Their fear was gone, but their distrust of Ben was still firmly in place.

"I'm not surprised. What's the problem?"

Figures began marching across the screen: Ben's requested budget figures, projected outputs for various synthesized compounds, comparisons to other options, average return on investment for his and other departments, overhead allocations by department and project. Boring.

Ben had less and less tolerance for this kind of number dicing and slicing. They took real ideas from real people, exciting insights that might actually improve the human condition, and converted them to numbers. They monetized and emasculated genius until is was just so many bytes of date swirling in the machine, till all the life and inspiration were wrung out in the equation. It was soul-deadening and infuriating at the same time.

"Look," he said, interrupting the chairperson, "Let's cut to the chase, or get to the bottom line, or whatever cliché we're using this week."

He strode to the head of the table and grabbed the chairperson's handheld and stylus. He started drawing overlapping circles that showed up on the overhead screen.

"It's a simple Euler diagram. You saw them in school. You can have shock proteins or telomerase or betagamma72— whatever you want from my lab—you can have it fast, cheap, or good, but you can't have all three at the same time. Usually the best you can do is two out of three. Traditionally, ChemGen has gone for fast and cheap, using mostly harvested tissue fractions from actual humans, running poor people through body salons like pigs through a slaughterhouse, using everything but the squeal.

"When you pick fast and cheap, you don't get good. You have to lie about quality and call stem cells a hundred percent synthetic when they're only ten percent. This will work as long as you keep bribing the right people to keep your labeling loophole open, and as long as nobody blows the whistle in sensitive areas like the American south and makes a stink. When you pick fast and cheap, you take more risk. You risk contamination, subpar reactivity, latent pathogens, inconsistencies, and variability.

"Kalimer wants less exposure in this area. I'm showing you how you can expand the good circle enormously, go to as much as eighty percent synthetic. But it's going to be a little tiny bit more costly, or take a little longer. Why are you guys always so reluctant to go for the good? Don't you know your souls work the same way?" He drew another three circles:

"You can go for the money, you can go for integrity and ethics and be a good person, or you can go for freedom in your research or your sex life or whatever. But you can't have all three at once. Pick any two out of the three."

He tossed the pad and stylus to the chairperson. "You guys pick and let me know. I'm tired of watching you hash and rehash the numbers." He walked out.

He went back to the lab and cleared off a bench and laid down on it, palming his eye sockets and trying to slow his breathing and heart rate. He was flushed and feverish again. Behind his eyes he saw his circles and Euler diagrams. It had all come to him in a flash of clarity, like ideas appeared to him in his twenties, complete and whole and shining like gems. Surely they would see the light and approve his budget.

But no. His handheld chimed and he checked the message: *Committee requests you reduce your budget by 30%.*

That would put his department back to last year's numbers, preserving the status quo, and gutting most of his plans for improvement. Ben palmed his eye sockets again, pressing until he saw stars and fireworks.

27. Trim Tabbing

He started thumbing his handheld, composing a message to Kapoor at Kalimer:

Trujib: I have files and vmails and documents showing how you stole my research, how you tampered with the human trial data by moving prisoners around. I can prove your recent acquisitions and mergers constitute insider trading. I know that Kalimer is not just trying to vertically integrate the production of Rejuven. You're also trying to close off any possible whistle blowers by tying everyone like me up with nondisclosure clauses and debt blackmail. I can show how you shuffled me aside to cheat me out of patent and discovery bonuses.

You have two choices: Reinstate me as lead scientist on Rejuven in San Francisco, with full bonuses and patents. Or suffer the shitstorm of bad press I can unleash.

He knew what Louise would say. And Cynthia Lim and his old roommate and all the other company drones: Take it easy. Don't commit corporate suicide. Hunker down and don't draw attention to yourself. Play it safe. But he was sick of playing it safe. It was time to take a stand, to be daring and unconventional, to poke the tiger. He would be bold and canny, kick this thing into a higher orbit, raise the stakes.

He pushed the SEND and sent the message off to Kapoor. Let Trudge try to finesse this one. Let him try to cover over and sneak around and move behind the scenes in his perfect circles. He couldn't hide in the brassy gear train of the corporate orrery anymore. Ben Rasmussen would flush him out, expose the true ellipses of corporate greed and malfeasance.

Ben felt great after his orgasm of spleen. Maybe he would quit entirely, quit ChemGen and Kalimer and the whole corrupt machine. But no, he wasn't that crazy, not yet. He would work from inside the machine, manipulating and forcing it to work for the good, wherever and whenever he could make that happen. While still getting a decent paycheck, still living back in the states in his accustomed lifestyle. He would squeeze the Euler circles tighter together, create a pinprick point of balance in the middle of the shitstorm, where he could have it all: fast, cheap, rich, free, and above all Good.

In moderation, of course. It would be a masterful balancing act. He would have the resources and lifestyle and salary draw and prestige of a corporate science career, plus the intellectual freedom to pick and choose his projects, plus integrity. If turned out he couldn't have all three in equal measure, he would make judicious adjustments. Whereas he formerly had felt like an insignificant flea on the Kalimer elephant, he now felt that he could be the trim tab on the rudder of the Kalimer battleship, a small intrinsic part subtly steering it in a better direction. He fell asleep on the lab bench, exhausted and empty.

28. A Nanny Who Can Shoot

When he awoke it was dark outside and everyone had gone home. It was nearly midnight. ChemGen was a spooky place, haunted by the traces of its vanished inhabitants: a candy wrapper on a desktop screen, a scarf over the back of a chair, a hairbrush fallen to the floor. Ben picked up the hairbrush and smelled the bristles. Patchouli or some other earthy scent. It was a kind of human contact.

Bleary-eyed and woozy, he wandered outside and flagged down a cab. He had the cabbie stop at Mr. Tam's store on the way home. He picked up a bottle of Malay Jaz brandy. He and Glory could get loaded and have a little party.

But when he got home, Glory was in a bad mood. She was hunched over her handheld at the kitchen table, poking at the screen and sniffling.

"What's wrong," Ben asked.

"This damn site."

He looked over her shoulder. She was on some government site. U.S. Immigration Service, all tiny text and no icons, designed to confuse functional illiterates like Glory.

"Let me help you," he said. "What are you trying to do?"

"I'm trying to check and see if I got visas for me and Lilly."

"You're going to the states?"

"Yeah."

"When?"

"Whenever they let us in."

"Why wouldn't they let you in?"

She looked down. "These aren't tourist visas."

"What do you mean?"

109

"We almost have enough saved to fly to America and live with my sister Sylvia."

"To live? With a sister? I didn't even know you had a sister in the states."

Glory took a deep breath. "I didn't want to tell you, unless it really was going to happen. Sylvia won a big space in a housing mall in California. She's an artist and calls herself Anarcha or Antichrist or something like that. She doesn't like me to talk about her anyway."

"Why not?"

"She makes these bogus websites. You know those ones that look like real corporate sites? But the CEO's in drag, humping the American Eagle or the French Bullfrog?"

"I love those sites."

"Well, she's always getting in trouble, always being shut down. Nobody's supposed to know where she lives, but I do, and me and Lilly are gonna live with her there."

"When were you going to tell me?"

"When I had to."

Ben turned and went quickly into the bathroom and shut the door. Tears had sprung to his eyes, surprising him. The thought of Glory leaving hit him like a physical blow, right between the eyes, sudden and stunning as a punch. He had so quickly become attached to their days and nights together in this crummy apartment. These last weeks he had felt young again and in lust or love or whatever, drifting mindlessly through the golden hot afternoons, pounding up the stairs into the cool apartment, Lilly is off at school or something, Glory spread like a gift on the mattress on the teak flooring. He could smell Glory's smell, flowers and sweat and gun oil. It felt like the opposite of being married to Louise, free and easy and no strings. Until the strings pulled him up short.

His relationship with Glory didn't fit his old married topograph, the bisected parallelogram delineated by him and Louise and their two careers. Glory could hardly be said to have a career, and what there was of it involved protecting and taking care of Ben. Plus there was Lilly and the link, which made the whole arrangement feel more emotional, more organic, more like a water molecule. Glory was the foundation oxygen atom, deeply connected to and sustaining Ben and Lilly, the two hydrogen atoms. Life with Glory and Lilly flowed like water.

He wiped his eyes and took a deep breath, opened the door and returned to the kitchen.

"Here, he said, let me see that." Quickly he navigated to the correct page. "You need to sign in here. What's your user name?"

Together they worked through the clunky interface to a final positive outcome.

"See,... here... and here," Ben said, "You're approved. You've got the visas. You can pick them up at the consulate, or they'll mail them."

Glory hugged him. "Thanks. I'm sorry I didn't tell

you."

"It's okay. I might be moving back to San Francisco myself, if I can work it out. What's the plan? What will you do there?"

"Sylvia has a friend in San Bruno who needs a nanny who can shoot. That's me."

29. Too Small

Ben managed to get to work early. He was nervous because he had an appointment with Darius Jones from Kalimer Security.

"I just happened to be in town for a conference," Jones had said yesterday, "And Dr. Kapoor asked me to drop by and see you."

Nothing in Kalimer was that casual. People didn't just happen to be in town and people didn't drop by. Ben was nervous but curious as well. What could possibly prompt Kapoor to send one of their henchmen all the way over here. What could he have to say that couldn't be said in a v-mail?

Even though Ben was early, Jones was earlier. He was a big black man in a shiny black overvest, sitting on Ben's lab bench waiting for him after Ben unlocked the door.

"Dr. Rasmussen," he said, stretching out an enormous, well-manicured hand, "Darius Jones. Kalimer Security. We need to talk."

"Who let you in here?"

"No problem, I let myself in."

"Why did you come all the way from San Francisco? To see me?"

"No, as I said yesterday, I'm here at a conference. Dr. Kapoor wanted me to check in with you, go over a few things while I was in town."

"A few things like what?"

"It seems Kapoor is worried about you. He's worried that you might not understand the terms of your severance agreement."

"I think I understood everything. Kalimer dumped me just before the payoff on Rejuven. It's an old story." Ben put down the cup of chox he was holding, splashing some on the table, his hands were shaking so.

"Are you all right?" Jones said.

"No I'm not. I'm pissed off. Kapoor turfed me off to this hellhole, sold off my contracts to ChemGen like they were an entirely different firm. But what do you know, it turns out Kalimer owns a controlling interest in ChemGen. I'm still working for you assholes, in a way, except I've been bilked out of my rightful bonuses so Kalimer can save a few dimes and so Kapoor can subsidize his side squeeze, Cyn Lim."

"I see." Jones didn't seem fazed by Ben's outburst. Corporate Security types must have thicker skins than the executive caste.

"But that's just my story," Ben continued. "The bigger story is how Kapoor is mismanaging Rejuven. I've been watching InMates, and I also know how many prisoners have been transferred out of the trials, when their violent behavior on the drug gets then into trouble. There are ways to manage that, but I don't think Kapoor and Lim are up to it."

"And you are? Up to it?"

"I could be. Kapoor needs to put me back in charge of Rejuven trials, with a free hand."

"Do you really think that's going to happen?" Darius smiled with raised eyebrows. "When we put people out on waivers, they rarely come back."

"You need me back. For two reasons. Rejuven's in trouble, and I'm the guy who can fix it. It's a great drug, but it needs further refinement." Ben forced himself to clasp his hands tightly together and leave them in his lap, so Darius wouldn't see them shaking.

"You said two reasons. What's the second?"

"If I don't get back in charge, I'll go public with the whole mess. I have evidence that the press would love to see."

"What sort of evidence would that be?"

"Never mind that. You just need to know I have certain documents and information, and I'll willing to put it out there."

"I would not advise that," Jones said. "You must be aware of the nondisclosure agreement you signed, and of the laws about disgruntled employees. Don't forget what happened to the Dark Spotlight site, and those Wikileaks guys before them. You would be ruined."

"I don't care about myself. The world needs Rejuven, a good working formula. If they can't get it, people need to know why."

"I see." Jones went quiet again. He adjusted the fall of his black overvest, rubbed his hands together, and folded them neatly over his stomach. He had very large hands.

"And you can tell Kapoor that." Ben said.

"I certainly will." Jones rose and shook Ben's hand warmly. "Thank you for sharing your views so frankly," he said. He opened the door, then turned back briefly.

"Dr. Rasmussen?" he said.

"Yes?"

"Have you ever heard the catch phrase too big to fail, as applied to firms like Kalimer?"

"Of course."

"Perhaps you should also consider the corollary, as it applies to yourself."

"Which is?"

"Too small to succeed."

30. Boss Say No Talky

In the trishaw on his way home that night, Ben was surprised when the runner stopped dead in the road. Two young boys wearing bright pink linksets and tunics printed with cartoon characters had halted the cab and were directing the runner to turn down an alley.

"No," Ben said to the runner, "Don't turn here. What are you doing?"

In the alley the two young boys removed their link sets and placed them carefully on the lid of a dumpster. Then they pulled Ben from his seat like a sack of laundry and slammed him up against a tin wall. It rang like a gong and Ben's head rang too. He was dazed and had trouble separating the two sounds, one inside and one outside.

"Old man," one boy said, bunching his fists in Ben's overvest and leaning in close, talking up into his face from just an inch or two away. Ben could see that it was not a boy, but a young man, skinny but strong.

"Old man, you listen," the boy man said. "Boss say no talky. You keeping quiet."

Fire bloomed in Ben's stomach and he realized that the boy had punched him. He couldn't breathe. The boy let go and Ben slid to the ground. The other boy kicked him in the side and fire bloomed again. Ben's eyes went all watery and he curled into a ball. He felt them tugging at his pants and his wallet and handheld came free. He heard their footsteps retreating down the alley. Not even running, just walking away with no hurry. Sauntering.

Ben lay on the gritty pavement for a long time, until his head stopping spinning and the boys and the trishaw were long gone. No one came down the alley. He was alone. The alley seemed curiously quiet for K.L. The busy street sounds were muted and far away. Ben didn't feel so much younger and stronger anymore. He felt every day of his sixty years and then some. Very slowly he got to his hands and knees. His stomach lurched and squirmed and he threw up, splashing his hands. Finally he levered himself slowly to his feet. His stomach and ribs were sore, and his knees and hands were scraped raw. He wiped his wet hands on his shirt.

The violence had shaken him deeply. It was so much different from the movies. He felt drained and exhausted. How did those movie heroes jump up from a fight and run into the next scene? Ben felt like he could barely walk. He shuffled along the alley, one hand half supporting him against the tin siding. When he got to the main street, he looked for a taxi, then remembered that he had no wallet, no phone, no credit cards or UN dollars. He'd have to walk the rest of the way home. Maybe Glory would have some bandages for his knees.

He had about two miles to go, but it seemed much longer in the heat and his depleted condition. "I'm in shock," he said to himself several times over, "I'm in shock." The sun hurt his eyes and they teared up constantly. He realized that he had lost his sunglasses somewhere too. He felt disoriented and somehow detached from his own alien body. The teeming streets seemed unreal. Nobody would make eye contact with him, this tall white guy limping and gimping along the sidewalks.

31. Bubbles

It took him over an hour to reach his familiar neighborhood. By then he felt a little better and had started to think again. It seemed likely that Darius Jones had turned the two young toughs on him. He'd never prove it, but it made sense. That was fast work on Jones' part, and revealed a network of connections in K.L. that you had to admire. It was an extreme move for Jones to take, desperate perhaps, but safe enough. People were roughed up all the time in a big city. Who would think a big outfit like Kalimer would stoop to such tactics?

The gate to the courtyard was ajar. He'd have to give Glory some shit about that. Jenkins would be livid if he saw the gate open. Ben closed and latched it.

The lobby was empty too. Glory's student desk was lying on its side, her handheld on the floor. Alarmed, Ben called out, "Glory? Are you here?" He righted the desk and picked up the handheld.

No answer. He ran up the stairs to his apartment, and that door at least was firmly locked. As he put in his key, he heard Lilly crying inside. He opened the door and rushed in. Glory was lying on the living room floor in a pool of blood, and Lilly was sitting on the couch crying.

"Help her, she's hurt," Lilly said.

Ben knelt by Glory's head. She had a small hole in her chest but all the blood was coming from underneath her somewhere. She opened her eyes and saw Ben.

"He shot me," she said. "Young punk with a revolver. Did you see him?"

"Nobody out there. Lie still."

"He came through the window. Lilly was here studying. I heard her scream and came up as fast as I could. But he shot me, the bastard."

"Be quiet, don't talk. I'm calling an ambulance. He fumbled for his handheld, but he didn't have it. He said to Lilly, "Get on your 'vice and call 911, or whatever you call here for emergencies."

Lilly said through her tears, "I already called. Mom put it on my speed dial. The ambulance is coming, and the cops."

Glory grabbed Ben's arm, fingers digging into the flesh. "Ben, pay attention. This is bad, this is serious. If anything happens to me, take care of Lilly."

"Don't talk like that. You're going to be fine."

She shook her head and grimaced in pain. Ben saw the edge of the pool of blood move outward a little. He thought they should turn her over, apply pressure or something.

Glory squeezed his arm tighter. "Take Lilly to Sylvia's," she said, "It's all set up."

"Quiet," Ben said. "Just try to relax and hang on. You're going to be okay."

But she wasn't. She smiled up at him and then just went away, like a computer entering sleep mode, a machine turning off. Her eyes were open still, but her hand fell away from his arm and he heard one last gurgle in her throat, then nothing.

He pushed his fingers into her neck, trying to check for a pulse like on TV, but he knew she was gone, just like that. He couldn't remember what to do in what order, something about clear the airway, pinch the nose, tilt the head back. Lilly was crying louder on the couch, making it harder to think.

He got on his knees by Glory's head, kneeling on her hair.

"Sorry," he said automatically. He tipped her head back and her mouth opened. It looked clear, so he pinched her nose shut and breathed into her mouth. Her chest didn't rise like it was supposed to. The hole in her chest blew a blood bubble and Ben felt like he might throw up again. He thought about that pushing thing, compressions, but he's have to place his hands on top of the bloody wound. That couldn't be right. He kept doing the mouth to mouth, but all that happened was more bubbles.

He was dithering, shaking blood off his hands, straightening Glory's limbs, trying to think of what to do, when someone poked his arm. It was a woman in white coveralls, wearing rubber gloves and a face mask.

She said something in Malay, then in English, "Move, move."

Pushed aside, Ben sat with Lilly on the couch and watched the woman in white and a man work over Glory with tubes and bags and plastic things. After a while the woman got up and touched Ben on the arm.

"Sorry, she is gone. Can you take little girl out?"

Ben and Lilly went into the bedroom and sat on the bed, hugging her close.

"Is she dead?" Lilly said.

"I'm sorry, baby, she is."

"She can't be."

"She is."

After another space of time, he could never remember how long, or what else they said to each other on the bed, if anything, Lilly was shaking his arm.

"Benny... Benny... The police are here."

A police woman stayed with Lilly in the bedroom and a police man took Ben to the lobby and asked him what happened. He tried to explain about Trujib and Jones and getting mugged and how it was all connected, but it didn't seem to be getting across to the officer.

The two medical techs came through the lobby pushing a stretcher. For a moment, Ben didn't realize that the long white bundle on the stretcher was Glory's body. It seemed so small, so anonymous. He watched it float out through the open front door into blinking blue lights, feeling again like he was in a movie.

The officer asked Ben to hold out his hands. Ben did and the officer sprayed them with something cold from a can. He shined a small flashlight on Ben's hands, and made a note in his notebook.

"You not fire gun today."

Ben felt a ridiculous wave of relief.

The officer closed his notebook and handed Ben a card.

"You come here, you and Lilly Banks, tomorrow. Nine of the clock. Sign statements."

32. "Don't Leave Me"

Ben and Lilly couldn't stay in the apartment with the bloody rug. They went to Lilly's tent and crawled inside. The tent still held the heat of the day, but they sat close together anyway on Lilly's sleeping bag, arms around each other and Lilly half on Ben's lap. They sat like that for a long time, Lilly crying and Ben rubbing her shoulder.

Lilly wiped her eyes and asked, "What will happen to

her?"

"The police doctor has to . . . examine her."

"Autopsy."

She was so smart. "Yes, I suppose. Then we'll have a funeral. A ceremony of some sort."

"Like Popsie."

"Popsie?"

"Our cat that died. We buried her in the garden with her mousie."

"Yeah, like Popsie."

"But not in the garden?"

"No, probably not. And no mousie."

She giggled. A very short, very unhumorous giggle. She rolled away from Ben and snuggled into her pillow. In a sleepy underwater tone she asked, "Will the police find the guy who shot her?"

"I hope so." He wanted to strike out at someone, blow someone away. But there was no one there but he and Lilly. The guy who shot Glory was obviously looking for Ben's supposed evidence. He had to make Kalimer pay for this somehow.

Ben thought Lilly was asleep, but she opened her eyes and said, "Am I staying with you now?"

"Sure," he said, but thought for how long? Forever?

"Okay, but I'm going to sleep here tonight."

"That's fine."

"You sleep here too?"

"Yes, I'll stay right here."

"Tomorrow we can live in the apartment, but not tonight."

"Okay."

"Don't leave me."

"I won't."

Lilly closed her eyes. Ben lay back on Glory's sleeping bag. It smelled like her. The light dimmed outside and the fabric of the tent shifted from orange to brown to black. He felt ashamed and stupid. It was all his fault for involving Glory and Lilly in his troubles. In his ersatz youthful enthusiasm, he thought he could blow the whistle and fix everything. He threatened to expose Kalimer with evidence he really didn't have, unwisely poking the corporate tiger and tipping his hand. If he hadn't threatened Kalimer, this wouldn't have happened. It was a mess and he didn't know what to do.

33. Resolution of Open Accounts

The tent was glowing orange again when Ben woke up. His stomach muscles and lower back felt stiff and sore where he had been punched. The horrible events of yesterday flooded his mind like flushing a toilet. Glory's murder, the mugging, Kalimer. He cautiously arched his back and kneaded his abs. He actually had abs now, instead of a little paunch, and he knew the soreness would fade soon. Before Rejuven, he would have been wincing for a week, but now he healed faster, shaking off small physical insults like a younger man.

He reached automatically for his handheld to check the time. In his pocket he found Glory's instead. His was gone in the mugging.

He turned Glory's 'vice on and saw the familiar field of sunflowers on her home screen. Lilly raised up on her elbow.

"That's Mom's"

"I know. I lost mine. Do you know her password?"

"lillydilly."

He thumbed it in and checked his mail. A terse text message from Human Relations at ChemGen read:

Dear Doctor Rasmussen:

Due to your absence from regularly scheduled meetings,

your unauthorized time off, your personal use of company equipment, your dereliction of duty, and other violations of your employment contract, detailed in file 12489/vitae/ Rasmussen, we are exercising our right of termination as of noon today. Please see Debt Counselor Ms. Fatima Bintafu in the Human Relations Department for release of personal effects and resolution of open accounts.

"What's wrong," Lilly asked.
"I'm too small."
"Huh?"
"To succeed."

34. "What's Going to Happen to Me?"

The neighborhood police station was small, noisy, and chaotic. Ben and Lilly waited nearly an hour to see the police inspector from yesterday and a new female cop. Lilly signed her statement about the stranger coming in the window, grabbing her, Glory rushing in, the man shooting her mom, Ben coming in soon after.

The cops seemed suspicious and bored at the same time. Ben felt like he was a suspect, even though Lilly's story placed him at the apartment after Glory was shot, even though his hands were free of gunpowder residue.

Ben signed his statement, after trying to explain again about Darius Jones' threats and his conviction that the killer was searching his apartment for work papers. The cop reluctantly changed a few words on the form and Ben initialed them, but they didn't seem very interested in pursuing that line of inquiry.

"Most likely burglar," the female officer said. "You live in very bad neighborhood."

"Somebody looking for drugs, maybe," the male cop said. Ben wondered if they had seen his stash of Rejuven.

Ben said, "I tell you, they were looking for evidence damaging to ChemGen and Kalimer. Find Darius Jones, he's the one behind this."

"We check with ChemGen personnel, they have no Mr. Jones."

"He's from Kalimer, I told you. From San Francisco. He's why I got fired today." Ben held up Glory's computer.

They just smiled and looked at him. The male officer held up his notebook, to indicate that he had written down Jones' name and would follow up, all in good time.

Ben was sweaty and his hands were shaking. His heart was pounding and he could feel it as a deep dull throb in his aching head. His rumpled clothes hung on his frame, he had lost so much weight recently. He realized that he must be the very picture of a Disgruntled Ex-Employee, a Substance Abuser, a Poor Prospect, too small to succeed, blaming all his trouble on some mythical corporate killer from America.

"What about Glory's body," he asked. "When can we arrange for a funeral?"

"After autopsy," the male cop said, flipped through a clipboard. "she will be... sorry, says here... Release to organ contract holder."

He turned the clipboard around so they could see.

"What does that mean?" Ben asked.

"Oh yeah," Lilly said, "I forgot."

"Forgot what?"

"There's nothing to bury," Lilly said. "Once when we were really broke, mom and I went to the organ site and signed this organ donor thing."

Ben felt shocked. It must have shown in his face, because Lilly went on, "No it's fine. Mom said other people could use our spare parts. It's helping people. And we needed the money. They paid in UN dollars."

Ben said. "Sure, honey, I see. Of course, it's fine. I was

just surprised. We can still have a ceremony, a memorial."

He tried to change the subject by asking the policeman, "What about Lilly? What will happen to her?"

"She has family? Father?"

"An aunt in California."

"Best she can go to aunt. If not, there is orphanage or work home."

That didn't sound good to Ben. That didn't sound like what Glory had in mind when she asked him with her dying breath to take care of Lilly.

"I'll call her aunt," he said. "She can stay with me until we figure something out."

The cop shrugged. "We call you if we find anything." He began gathering his papers and stood up, indicating that the interview was over. He ushered Ben and Lilly out of the room and into the noisy lobby.

On the way out of the police station, Lilly asked, "What's going to happen to me?"

"I can call your aunt. What's her name?"

"She's Aunt Sylvia, Mom's sister in California. But I don't know her. I never met her."

"If she's half as nice as your mom, you'll be fine." Ben thumbed Glory's handheld and found Sylvia, no last name, and a v-mail address.

"I want to stay with you," Lilly said.

"I won't be staying here. I don't have a job anymore. I'll have to move."

"Where?"

"Back to the states, I guess. That's where my wife is. My ex-wife I mean."

"So you could stay here with me, if you want to."

"I never wanted to come here in the first place."

"Oh."

"But I'm glad I did. I got to meet your mom, and you, and that's been great."

They walked slowly in the heat toward a taxi stand.

"I'll call your aunt this afternoon," Ben said. "It's still late at night in California."

35. Memorial

The memorial for Glory was simple. Lilly moved all her stuff into Ben's apartment, and turned the tent into a shrine, arranging some of her mom's favorite things on her sleeping bag: a photo of Glory and Lilly and Ben at the park, her ukulele, her link, and a worn stuffed kangaroo.

They sat in the tent, linked together. Lilly played some music with heavy subsonics, skirling bagpipes, and vague lyrics.

"This is Anthem Fantastique," she said, "By Blinkem. It's the only one of my songs I found on her 'vice. It had 122 plays, and I never knew she even liked Blinkem."

She choked up and started crying softly.

They had planned to each say something about Glory, but Lilly couldn't say anything but "goodbye," choked out between sobs.

Ben said, "Goodbye Glory. You were the best of us. You brought out the best in us. We will remember you and miss you forever."

Lilly laid down on the sleeping bag among the memorabilia, still crying. It was hot and stuffy in the tent, even in the shade of the banyan tree. Ben scooted alongside and rubbed her back. Lilly's crying got quieter and quieter. He kept rubbing her back. After a while he leaned over to see that her eyes were closed and she was asleep.

Ben sat there in the hot tent, sweat beading on his brow, sweat trickling between his shoulder blades. The murmur of K. L. traffic blended with Lilly's breathing. He stopped rubbing her back and started pulling blond hairs off of Glory's pillow. He wished he had kept a lock of her hair, put it in a golden reliquary like some Romantic hero. Her body and all her loose hairs and her hair brush and sandals and everything she was and had accumulated in thirty short years would now start dispersing, breaking down, being acquired and repurposed by others, dissolving into time, thinning and dimming and finally fading to nothing. Perhaps her kidneys or her heart would soldier on a few more years in someone else. But eventually all would be gone except memory, his and Lilly's and her sister Sylvia.

And then memory would fade. How long until the last shred of Glory was gone? Ben remembered the museum display from Lilly's field trip that he and Glory had glimpsed through her link. Some Mesopotamian beauty three thousand years ago shaped a pot that cracked and was tossed into a desert midden, to be found later by some archeologist, examined and cataloged and put on display in a glass case, to be idly scanned by a camera in a schoolgirl's link and transmitted to her mom, who showed her boyfriend, who now thought of that almost forgotten potter one more time. It was the wispiest kind of immortality, the memory of a trace of a long-gone shaping hand.

Lilly mumbled in her sleep. He rubbed her back some more and she calmed down. Glory would live on in Lilly, in a way, sort of. Half her DNA anyway, and some mannerisms — her sudden laugh, the way she tossed her hair back, how she'd touch you lightly with one finger to get your attention. He could almost feel her touch now, but that would fade. Her DNA would dilute in Lilly's children and her children's children. That was the traditional consolation, but it was thin stuff, not enough to cushion the hard black rock of Glory passing into oblivion.

He stretched his arms and rolled his shoulders, feeling his biceps flex against his shirt. His own body would be dust eventually too. His muscles were a little larger and firmer these days, thanks to Rejuven's cellular accelerators. The training effect was easier to achieve, even with just normal activity levels. But his stronger muscles were also a little uncoordinated, a little prone to twitches and trembles and random cramps. Nerve tissue didn't like to be accelerated. And what did it matter, any-how, if he made his corpus last a few years longer? Considering how long he would be gone and forgotten in the grand organ recycling scheme under the soil?

He took off his link and stretched out on Glory's mat, squeezing next to Lilly, and looked up at the tent fabric dappled with blurry coins of sunlight. A mosquito bit him on the cheek and he slapped it, smearing bug juice and his own blood into the tears that had silently leaked out his eyes and into his ears. Another death. Another small life gone.

He felt asleep and dreamed of pursuing Glory across a frozen river breaking up in spring. Giant blocks of ice cracked loose and went floating away in thunderous silence. He clam-bered from one shifting block of ice to another, in hideous slow motion, barely able to move, while the block Glory was on drift-ed away faster than he was moving. She was smiling at him and saying something, but he couldn't hear her over the silence of the thaw.

He crawled on his hands and knees, looking down at the fissured ice and seeing grand canyons of white and gray and blue that he was flying over in his plane. He circled the plane over the frozen landscape, but could not find the airport where he was supposed to rendezvous with Glory. He had to find it and land before his fuel was gone, but he was flying over a barren artic landscape with no airstrip or flat place to land.

The plane's engine began sputtering and thumping, making a weird scraping sound that was impossible for a jet to make. He realized that he was awake, in Glory's tent, and the scraping was coming from outside.

Lilly wasn't next to him.

"Lilly?" Ben called, "Is that you?"

"Yeah, just a minute." It sounded like Lilly was digging earth from under the tent floor. Ben was just about to go outside and see what was going on when the scraping stopped and Lilly came back into the tent.

"I dug up this for you," she said. She handed him a small

tin biscuit box. "It's Mom's safe."

Ben opened the box and found it full of UN dollars and two passports.

"She was saving to fly to the USA," Lilly said. "We got the passports and everything."

"It looks like a lot of money." He counted the small multicolored bills.

"See, I can pay my own way. I can pay for your ticket too. So you got to take me with you when you leave."

"We'll see," Ben said. "Money's not the only problem." But it's a very big part of the problem, he thought, as usual.

They were both wide awake now. Lilly handed Ben the handheld.

"Read to me."

He opened up the Harry Potter book, and started to read, using different voices for Harry and Dumbledore and Hermione and the rest.

"Don't forget this," Lilly said, handing him the link. Ben put it on without missing a beat, and they settled back into the life at Hogwarts.

At the end of a chapter, Lilly nudged him with her foot and said, "If you take me to the USA, we can read all the Harry Potter books together."

"I know. I'd like that."

Part Three

36. Counterfeiters

"It matters not what someone is born, but what they grow to be," Ben read from Harry Potter and the Goblet of Fire. He pitched his voice just above the whine of the 787's engines so Lilly could hear, but not loud enough to bother anyone else, he hoped.

"Highlight that one," Lilly said.

Ben dutifully highlighted the sentence.

"You love Dumbledore," he said. "over half your quotes are from him."

"So what? I can't help it if J. K. gave all the good lines to him."

"You're just a sucker for a magical father figure."

She shrugged. Ben turned off his handheld and massaged his eyes.

"I've got to stop reading for a while," he said. "I'm getting queasy."

"Okay," Lilly said. "I'm going to the loo."

"You just went ten minutes ago."

"I don't really have to go, silly." She poked him in the arm. "I just like the restroom. It's so teeny." She popped up into the aisle and wandered to the back of the plane.

The woman in the window seat to Ben's left said, "You're daughter is adorable. She's so well-behaved."

"Thank you," Ben said. "Her mom gets all the credit, though."

"No, you're great with her."

"Well, thanks for saying." Ben was pleased that she thought Lilly was his daughter, and content to leave it at that. The whole long story of why they were flying to San Francisco together was too complicated and too sad to lay out for a stranger.

His stomach was upset. The whine and vibration of the plane's engines seemed to irritate his very bones. His joints ached. He squirmed in the cramped coach seat and tried to get comfortable. He seemed to have less leg room than on the trip over to K. L. and he made a mental note to measure himself. It was quite possible that synovial deposition had actually made him a little taller, the shock absorbing cartilage lining each joint becoming just a tiny bit thicker. It would add up. From age twenty to eighty the average person lost and inch and a half of height. Rejuven might give him back as much as an inch.

But it wasn't comfortable. He looked longingly forward to first class with its roomy seating. He had to be very careful with money. He had cashed in his ex-wife Louise's unused first class ticket to K. L. to pay for his and Lilly's coach fare. It wasn't quite enough, and he had reluctantly borrowed from the UN dollars Glory had saved and stashed away in the biscuit tin under the floor of their tent.

He turned on his handheld and made a lab note: Maybe I should think of my aching joints as "growing pains," as in "growing younger pains." Probably just local inflammation from the cellular accelerators.

The woman next to him was watching the news and he caught sight of the Kalimer logo. He turned up his own audio:

...vealed today that three of the top ten drugs on the latest Merck Index of Street Drugs are counterfeit versions of Kalimer's forthcoming anti-aging pill Rejuven. Asked

about the prerelease buzz about Rejuven, Kalimer repre-
sentatives insisted that they have not circulated any sneak
previews of the drug, and that the official release date is
still pending final approval of its human trials, scheduled
for later this year. They warned against unsupervised rec-
reational use of any drug, and promised to vigorously pros-
ecute all counterfeiters of its proprietary formulations.

He stared at the screen for while, but there was no more about Rejuven. He turned it off. Maybe Kapoor was afraid that Ben himself would try to counterfeit Rejuven and sell a street version. Ben would never do that, even if it were possible for one scientist to put together an exact reproduction of the drug. But he could easily see Kalimer paranoia about the prospect of counterfeiting. The real drug's side effects were daunting enough. Just imagine the havoc a fake version might play.

He went back to the notes on his 'vice screen, but he couldn't think of anything more to write, so he turned that off too. He wished he had the paper notes from his lab at ChemGen. But he'd left them behind, hidden in the lab where he couldn't get at them. When he had gone to retrieve his belongings from Chem-Gen, his key no longer opened his office or lab, and security told him that he could pick up his stuff in Human Relations. He headed off in that direction, but swerved at the last moment and left the building. He'd never get his stuff without talking to the debt counselor first, and he didn't want to start that ball rolling. That way led to bankruptcy and ruin, so let them come find him. He wasn't going to stick his own neck in the chopper.

Lilly came back. "Still queasy?" she asked.

"Yes, a little." He passed her the handheld. "You read the next chapter to me."

"But I'm so slow."

"That's all right. This is how you get faster."

37. Green and Glossy

The front door of Ben's old house was freshly painted black. Louise had been after him for over a year to get it painted. He never would have chosen black. It opened and Louise stood before them. She was thinner, slim even, and wearing a clingy silk top with a chic linen overvest. She must still be dressed for work. She looked cool and corporate and cross.

She swung the door wider and stood aside, still holding the doorknob. "Come in, I guess."

Ben and Lilly entered the foyer. He could smell the fresh roses on the antique hall table. They stood in the center of the hall runner, Lilly sticking close to Ben and inspected Louise intently.

"I'm sorry to do this to you," Ben said, "I hate to ask you to put us up. But I just don't have any other choice. We can't afford to go to a hotel."

"We're not even married anymore," Louise said, "and you show up on my doorstep with a little girl?"

"She's not so little. She's eleven, and she's used to taking care of herself."

"Almost twelve," Lilly put in, "in April."

Louise finally closed the door. "Well come on in anyway, for while, but this is not okay with me."

She led them into the great room. Ben saw that there was some new furniture and appliances and that everything had been re-arranged. It didn't look like his house anymore. Lilly's eyes got big as she took in the clean, modern, all matching furniture, the spacious foyer and open plan living/dining area, the kitchen with its gleaming stainless steel and highly polished granite countertops. But she didn't say anything, just drifted to the Doric column flanking the entry to the sunken lounge area and put her back up against it.

As Ben came out of the dim entryway and into the light of the lounge. Louise got a good look at him for the first time, and she gasped.

"Ben, what's happened to you?"

"I'm taking my own drug."

"You look so different. Younger. Kind of." She reached out and touched his face, gingerly like touching a stranger's dog.

"I am younger, kind of. It's the Rejuven, the drug I worked on for so long."

"It's amazing. What does it feel like?"

"Like being a teenager again, full of fizz." He bumped her hip with his playfully, and she shied away.

"Did you dye your hair?"

"No, it just grew in brown again."

"Thicker too." She circled around him, checking out his body like a used car she was dubious about, but might buy anyway, if the price was right.

"You've lost weight too."

"More like put it in different places. More muscle, less fat." He flexed his biceps in a Charles Atlas pose and grinned at her.

On the sidelines, Lilly rolled her eyes and sighed. "Where's the loo?" she said.

Ben pointed down the hall. "First door on the left." Lilly left the room.

Louise motioned Ben to a chair and they sat down.

"Lilly's mom died?" she asked.

"Yeah, she was killed. It was my fault, in a way. I promised to look after Lilly, get her settled with her aunt in San Bruno."

"You and her mom…"

"We… got together in Malaysia."

"You didn't waste any time."

"I guess not, but you were the one who wanted the divorce, not me. I was faithful to you all the time we were married, so don't give me a hard time about Glory."

"Glory?"

"Gloria Banks. Glory B for short. She's Australian. Was Australian."

"Blond?"

"Yes."

"Younger than me."

"True, but not her fault."

"No, it's your fault. Did you love her?"

"Louise, please."

"Sorry."

She got up and paced to the sideboard, grabbed a bunch of keys and tossed them into his lap.

"Here. You guys can stay here tonight, but tomorrow you have to go. You can stay in the lake house. I haven't been going out there much. You might as well make use of it."

"Thanks, Louise. I appreciate it."

"It's not for you. It's for the girl."

"Lilly."

"Right, it's for Lilly. Not for Glory B."

Later, after Lilly had gone to sleep, Ben and Louise were sitting in the lounge area, on opposite ends of the leather couch, sipping red wine.

"You were right to dump me," Ben said, "You could see I was heading for a fall, and I couldn't see it myself."

"That's not why I was unhappy. I don't care about the job."

"But I do. I did. I have this tunnel vision or blinders that make focus on my research and ignore everything else. I get obsessed, work too much, neglect my wife, my health."

"That much is true. You neglected me. And I neglected you right back."

"I marvel at reasonable people, people who can step

back, evaluate whether a course of action or line of research is worth pursuing, and then allocate a reasonable amount of time each week to devote to it. But that's not how I operate."

"I know. I'm the same way, all or nothing. What's it like, being on the drug?"

"It's a mixed bag. In general, it's good. I'm stronger, more energetic. Most of the time my mind is clear and I can come up with better ideas, more imaginative notions. Sex is amazing."

"Thanks for sharing that."

"Sorry, but it's true." He laughed.

"Rejuven is a stupid name. Sounds like street talk: 'We be rejuvin, baby!'"

"I know. I refuse to take the blame for the name. They didn't even ask me for my ideas. 'Rejuven' makes it sound so green and glossy, but it's not all roses. I get depressed, or pissed off, really easily. Mood swings I can't control. I'm more impulsive, like I was when we first met."

"I'd like to try it."

"No, I can't do that. I shouldn't have taken it myself. It's a violation of all kinds of rules."

"Young people don't care about the rules. Are you going to Bogart all the good drugs, just like you did in college?"

"That's not it. I have some shreds of maturity and judgment left. It would be unethical to give you Rejuven. The side effects are too unknown, too scary."

"What side effects?"

"Headaches, high blood pressure, tremors. It's a real freak show."

"Are you all right?" She put her hand on his knee.

"I don't know. Not yet." He put down his wine and moved closer to her and took her hand. "Believe me, I don't think Rejuven is ready for prime time. Not yet." He kissed her. She kissed him back.

38. Mind Clicking

Ben and Lilly drove an electric two seater from the CarPool down to San Bruno to meet her aunt Sylvia. In the car Lilly's dam of silence broke and she started to speak:

"I've never met aunt Sylvia. That sucks. My mom never even took me to see her, and now I'm going to get dumped on her."

"I'm not dumping you anywhere. We're just going to meet her, see what the situation is. Your mom thought enough of her sister to want to emigrate and live with her. That should tell you something."

"Mom was clueless. She couldn't even bring herself to fire that gun, and it got her killed."

"That's not fair."

"Life's not fair, Ben. Get used to it."

"I'm the adult. I'm supposed to tell you that."

"Adults, hah. You're all clueless."

"How so?"

"Take the link, for instance. Adults think links are a way to make music and sex better. They don't get that links are a new sense, like sight or hearing or taste. I'd have mine surgically implanted in my brain if I could. Nothing is better than roleplaying with your friends, all linked up and creating your own world faster than any single one of you can think on your own. Linking with a good friend is like opening up a direct channel to their heart and mind and soul."

"We adults didn't grow up with them the way you did."

"Some adults are good with the link. Mom used to link up with me and tell me stories at bedtime. It was the best."

"Better than when we link up and read to each other? You like Harry Potter a lot."

"Yeah, but that's a text book. Mom and me made up our

own stories. You didn't have to work to read them."

"When you get faster at reading, it doesn't seem like work."

"I'll never get that fast. I like icons. I don't get why you're hung up on text. It's backward."

"Text has been around thousands of years. The computer and the link were invented just yesterday, by comparison."

"So old is better, automatically?"

"No, I'm not saying that. I'm saying writing and reading have been around a long time, and they're not going away any time soon."

"I hate writing and reading. When I used to use your old 'vice, I'd feel all tongue-tied. That text-only keyboard was way too slow, punching out words. I prefer icons, they're so much more intuitive."

"You know they call that functional illiteracy, right?"

"So what? You just hear 'illiterate' and it freaks you out. I hear 'functional' and I'm green with that. That means I can function, right? That's the important part."

"I'm just saying that icons and logos and avatars are not a complete replacement for real language."

"Words are part of what got us into this mess. Simple logos are safer. Icon identification is even taught in school, so it must be the wave of the future. I can run a proper 'vice faster than you or my mom already."

"I have to admit, you are fast, with that mind-clicking."

"You could do it, if you tried."

"I tried once, but I couldn't get the hang of it. It gave me a headache."

"You have to keep practicing. It's hard at first, but then you get better. You got to be real precise with your eye movement, and subvocalize at just the right time. I can mind-click, mind-scroll, and sometimes I can mind-zoom."

"it just seems like a lot of trouble, to have to put on your link, wait for it to entrain, then use your thoughts to control a computer. When you have two perfectly good hands."

"If you're a kid, your link is always in sync anyway. Mind-clicking is like having a third hand."

"You kids look like zombies when you're mind-clicking, completely spaced out."

"We're in a far, far better place than the adult world."

Ben shrugged. "Whatever."

"Right, whatever." She poked him in the side playfully and he smiled.

39. The Maul

Ben wheeled the two-seater into Tanforan Estates, weaving among potholes, clutches of raised garden beds, bocce courts, and the occasional gasser motorhome, permanently parked up on blocks by high gas prices and carbon restrictions. They parked in the visitor lot among a small group of electric zippers, scooters, and trikes.

He had a vague memory of shopping there with his grandparents when he was a little kid. Back then it was still the age of Category Retail, when there were millions of privately owned vehicles and cheap gas to run them. Tanforan Estates was called Tanforan Mall, a fancy shopping center with acres of parking and dozens of large and small stores. His grandparents and parents and he would come to shop and eat and watch movies in the multiplex with their neighbors. It was a community cultural center and you felt like you belonged to the web of life when you strolled its warm and dry concourse, surrounding by music and potted palms. It was a more civilized and genteel time.

The mall was closed and partially flooded during the renovation of nearby San Francisco International Airport. After the runways were raised and the dike system completed, the old mall was pumped out. Tons of toxic mud were shoveled out by county work crews. Power and plumbing were restored. The old stores were remodeled and auctioned off as live/work condos. Ten percent of the spaces were designated low-income and put into the CalHab Lottery. Gloria's sister Sylvia won a 1,500 square foot space that had once been a Foot Locker—some kind of shoe store.

Approaching the former grand entrance, Ben saw that the exterior doorframes were empty of glass. No more air conditioning for the generous common areas. No more elders getting their exercise by mall-walking up and down the warm and dry concourse.

They walked over cracked terrazzo into the central atrium, dim and buzzing from dead and dying fluorescents. Ben could hear pigeons roosting way up in the ceiling. But the common atrium area was reasonably clean, and the walls were pied with six shades of off white, an admirable but doomed effort at graffiti control.

His handheld directed them up a stilled escalator with grime caked between the ribs of the steps. They went down a dark passageway and then into a larger area with skylights. There was a good-sized container garden under the skylights, with carrots, pea vines just starting to bloom, and lush lettuce. Ben's handheld showed that they had arrived at the coordinates Sylvia gave them. He dial her number.

Sylvia picked up on the first ring. "Ben?"

"We're here," he said.

"Yes, I can see you. Go down to the end of the hall to your right, and take the skyway across to building H. I'm in 2017."

A hundred yards further on, they arrived at Sylvia Banks' space, 2017, a narrow storefront with intact glass, spray painted white on the inside so you couldn't see in. A security gate was rolled down over the windows and door, then hacksawed out around the door.

They rung a brass bell screwed to the doorframe, and Sylvia Banks opened the door. She was shorter, thinner, and older than her sister Glory, but Ben could see the resemblance. She had the same blond hair, the same strong nose, the same direct gaze.

"Come on in." Her Aussie accent was fainter than Glory's. "I'm sorry for all the security, the coordinates and stuff, but I like to be careful about who comes here."

"I'm Ben, this is Lilly," Ben said.

"Sylvia." She shook hands with both of them, holding onto Lilly's hand. "Oh sweetie, you look just like Glory, just like your mom."

She pulled Lilly into an embrace, but Lilly was a little slow in raising her arms to hug back. Sylvia released her and stepped away, tears glistening in her eyes.

"Come along this way. We'll get comfortable and get acquainted."

She led them deeper into the old storefront. It had been remodeled with freestanding plywood partitions into a living area, two tiny bedroom cubicles, an office space with three old-school desktops hooked to wide panel screens, a kitchen like a galley on a ship with a propane stove, and a primitive bathroom.

"Welcome to my humble abode," she said. "I'm still kind of camping out here."

They sat in a collection of folding chairs and plastic lawn chairs around a low coffee table made from a hollow core door set on four ancient computer towers. Sylvia poured Ben some coffee from a thermos and got Lilly a soda.

"How long have you lived here?" Ben asked.

"Almost a year now. But it's so slow getting anything done. Until last month, I was still hauling water and going down to the concourse to shower. Now I'm tapped into the old sprinkler system for water, and they finally ran the sewer pipes upstairs, so I can flush my own jonnie."

Lilly looked around with big eyes. "It's nice," she said, sipping from her Sluice.

"Yes," Ben said, "Way nicer than your old tent. More

room." He looked around.

Sylvia pointed to the plywood wall behind Lilly. "The first bedroom is for Lilly. Before you go, maybe you could help me shove the wall this way a couple of feet. That will giver her more space."

"Sure," Ben said.

"I've wanted Glory and Lilly to join me in the states, for years. But I didn't have a good place to live, and neither of us could afford the fare or meet the immigration requirements. Then I won this place, and she saved up the fares and got their visas, and I thought our luck had changed." She grabbed a tissue from the table and wiped her eyes.

"Thank you," she said. "Thank you for getting Lilly over here, and for all you did for Glory."

"Glory was special to me," Ben said, "and so is Lilly."

"Where's her stuff? Did you leave it in the car?"

"Well, Lilly wanted to come down here and check out the situation first. Her stuff is still up in Santa Rosa."

"Oh." Sylvia balled up the tissue and rolled it between her palms.

"I feel kind of responsible for her," Ben said. "and we weren't clear about the situation."

"The situation?" Sylvia stared at Ben without blinking. Then she shut her eyes for what seemed like a long time. When she opened them she was looking upwards, at the ventilation ducts snaking across the ceiling. She lowered her gaze and spoke very slowly: "The situation is that I'm her aunt, she's my niece. We're family and we belong together. You seem like a nice man. Lilly's obviously comfortable with you. But I don't know you. Who are you, really? How long were you with Glory, anyway? And why did she get killed right after she took up with you? What did you have to do with that? You see, I'm pretty interested in checking out the situation myself."

"I know that you're family," Ben said, "but there's family and family. Especially since you guys have never actually met, is it appropriate for her to come live..."

"Appropriate? I can't believe this. There's no question she belongs with me. The real question is, who are you in all this?"

"I'm someone who cares about her."

"Don't fight," Lilly said, putting her hands over her ears. "Don't fight."

"Sorry, sweetie," Ben and Sylvia said simultaneously, both leaning towards Lilly. They exchanged looks.

Ben said, "Aunt Sylvia and I are just having a discussion." At that moment he felt that Sylvia was probably okay, that she was family, that she would be good for Lilly. But he needed more time to be sure.

"Let's take this one step at a time," he said. "Let's all get to know each other and get comfortable with the …situation. It's complicated."

'Fair enough," Sylvia said.

Lilly put her soda down on the table. "Ben," she said, "I want to go home."

"Okay Lilly, we'll be leaving pretty soon."

Things went all right from there. Sylvia was careful and courteous, Ben got quieter and more complimentary. Lilly was quiet and withdrawn. They parted with Sylvia on civil if not warm terms, saying they would talk more about the "situation" and figure things out later.

In the car, Lilly was clear: "That place freaks me out. It's bigger and nicer, but it's just a bigger and nicer tent. Your house is a real house. Your wife and you are nicer. Why can't I stay with you?"

"You can stay with me, for a while anyway. But Louise is my ex-wife, not my wife. And the houses are technically hers, not mine anymore."

40. Washing Glassware in a Clone Clinic

No one in the corporate sector would return his calls, much less give him an interview. When he did reach Roger, an old colleague in another pharmaceutical firm, Roger sounded flustered and scared, and feigned poor reception and cut him off. Ben was effectively blackballed and banned from working in corporate research.

It was infuriating and Ben resolved to get even. He would blow the whistle, tell all about Kalimer's shoddy human trials, their tampering with results, their use of mislabeled biological fractions in their drugs. He would bring civil and criminal charges. He would become a famous blogger and mobilize public opinion against Kalimer. He would be vindicated and he would bring them down.

In the meantime, he had to eat and buy hair clips for Lilly, so he looked for any job he could get. He ended up with exactly the job his old boss Trujib Kapoor threatened him with: washing glassware in a clone clinic. The only work he could find was at Marlene's Family Planning, a neighborhood clinic that did cloning, among other things. The pay was terrible, the hours only part time, the premises and equipment shabby and old.

"So Ben," Marlene said, handing him back his resumé, "Before you start you need to understand how the social service sector works."

"You're nonprofit, right?"

"Well, we don't turn any profit to speak of, but we're not nonprofit in the same way as big organizations like Purple Cross or Progressive Parenthood. They handle multicorporate people, people with health plans and the clerical staff to do their paperwork. We're not like Public Health, either. They handle the various flus and environmental endemics and stuff like that¬¬–sometimes. When there isn't any profit in it and¬ the multinationals let them. The social service sector handles the populations nobody else can make money on: the reservists on make-work jobs that don't feed them, the temps and illegals, the addicted and/or afflicted poor who can't afford state-of-the-art care."

"You make it sound pretty bleak."

"Yeah, I know. Sorry about that. My clinic's not so bleak. Here we serve a somewhat higher-functioning clientele. We provide proteomic health screening and family planning, so most of our people have got some kind of health awareness or family system going for them."

The work was routine, but Ben found it calming and satisfying in a way. He did a little of everything: Taking cheek swabs from clients and running them through the reader, devolving stem cells for patients with early Alzheimer's, screening ova and sperm samples for 176 possible genetic disorders, and, indeed, washing glassware from time to time. A high point of the first week was spotting a rare protein on a guy's scan that indicated his Huntington's sector was starting to express. The guy got into treatment quick enough to stop it.

Sometimes they had clients who wanted to design a baby from scratch, and he got to untangle their genomes and lay them out neatly into a plasmid. True cloning was pretty rare, but they did a lot of tweaking for those who needed fertility help or to dodge certain genetic bullets. The science was basic and well-established, but the applications were sometimes interesting, and usually made a difference for the better in people's lives.

Even washing glassware was not as emblematic of failure as Kapoor had maintained. You just popped it in the dishwasher and unloaded it later. Somebody had to do it.

41. What It Feels Like

"It's a trap. Get out!" Louise reached around Ben and hit the kill icon she'd set up. The handheld went dark.

"What's that, the fifth one?" Ben asked

"Fourth."

"I'd heard that some of the whistle-blowing sites were corporate fronts, but this is ridiculous."

"It is a little scary."

"You're sure they can't trace us?"

"Not geographically or digitally. But if you keep putting in references to Rejuven, they'll eventually figure out it's you. You're the most disgruntled employee in a small set."

Louise grabbed another handful of Shrinkles and took a swig of her red wine.

"Try the blog again," she said.

Ben fired up the handheld and tried to log onto their latest blog site.

"Damn, it's down already."

"What's it say?"

"Faulty protocol."

"Bullshit."

"Yeah."

"How long did this one last?"

"Six minutes."

"Well, that's a minute longer than last time."

"Whoopee."

Ben flopped back on the couch and rubbed his face, wincing at the acne on his chin. "This isn't going to work, is it?

She didn't say anything, just looked at him over her wine glass and shook her head minutely. Ben had started several blogs of his own, and tried ranting on other pharma blogs and forums. They had created bogus websites and held fake online press conferences. They impersonated Kalimer's R&D Division and issued "denials" of their own rumors. None of their efforts got any traction. They had all been effectively blocked by Kalimer's superior net apps, especially Google FireBreaks, that roamed the web and burned down any information detrimental to Kalimer's reputation.

Louise punched up a diagnostic screen. "My access is down to half speed," she said. "time to fire off another complaint to the ISP."

"I'm sorry," Ben said. He rubbed his eyes. His headaches were getting worse, especially when he spent any time staring at a computer screen. "This is a loosing proposition. Let's not do anymore. If I get any other ideas, I'll use another machine. It's not worth ruining your reputation."

"No problem. That's what this account is for. It's my throw-down piece. They'll shut down the speed until it's like wading through quicksand, then I'll cancel and open a new account. Have you had any word from the cops?"

"I finally got an appointment tomorrow with some detective in San Francisco. That's where the fraud squad is. But the lawyer said it's probably not going to get me anywhere to go criminal. Kalimer's contracts are too strong. And let's admit it, I signed them. I signed them every year, all those 'boiler plate' clauses, those 'formalities.' All those 'privacy notices' they send around every fifteen minutes. Who knew that 'non-response implies consent?'"

Ben slumped down on the couch. Something was under him and he squirmed to retrieve it—Lilly's spare link set. He held it out to Louise.

"Are you ready to try this yet?"

"I don't know. It seems so gimmicky and foreign."

"Just try it. There's nothing in here that isn't you."

She put it on. Ben picked his up from the coffee table and put it on.

"Now what do we do?" Louise asked.

"Nothing special. Just talk and hang out. You'll see. It's subtle."

"I don't know what to talk about. This is so artificial."

"Tell me a story. Something from when you were a kid. What did you like to do back then?"

"I don't know. Play I guess. Jump rope. And soccer later, and horseback riding. I liked to ride horses."

"Tell me about the horses."

"There was this place outside Stockton, an old landfill that they grassed over, where you could ride horses. Once a week after school my mom dropped me off there and I'd ride. My favorite was Silvertone. Horrible name for a horse, but I loved her."

"I had a guitar named Silvertone," Ben said. "Mine was brown. Was yours brown too?"

"Yes, with two white socks and a black mane and tale. I would draw pictures of Silvertone in school, and dream about him. Her I mean. Silvertone was a mare, but I always thought of her as a him."

As they talked, they made eye contact more often. They touched each other casually on the arm or knee. The links synchronized their brain waves, entraining rhythms and matching energy levels. The different sectors in their brains—memory, sense impressions, empathy and sympathy–lit up in tandem, and they became, ever so slightly, two parts of one organism.

"You look so different," Louise said, pushing back a lock of Ben's hair, "You even smell different." She nuzzled his neck. He rubbed her back, slipping his hand under her blouse.

"Ah, that feels so good. Is this what it feels like to be young?"

"Yes."

42. Complications

Lying in bed later, next to a sleeping Louise, Ben marveled at how easy it was to get into trouble. How easy it was to let his cock do the thinking, or more precisely the not-thinking. How familiar it felt these days to be so focused on sex and getting a woman into bed that the inherent practicalities and difficulties and negative consequences disappeared from view.

It was as if reality was a two dimensional Flatland, and arousal was a sudden translation into three dimensions, sticking up as it were, out of the dull quotidian plane, making it seem totally insignificant, overlookable. The biological imperative of the species expressed as pure geometric need.

Now that the hormone storm was over, he could see the drawbacks of bedding his ex. Did he really want to get back together, now? Because face it, she was still an old woman and he was a young man, comparatively. He could do so much better. He could attract and hold a younger, prettier woman like Glory or her sister Sylvia. He should check his sperm motility, see if Rejuven had done him any favors there. Should be up by twenty or thirty percent, if the prison trials were accurate in that regard and not just Kalimer foreshadowing plot developments in the next season of InMates.

This was more young man thinking, he realized. More young man not-thinking. More of the biological imperative leading him toward the greater reproductive opportunity. He was still following his genes around, dragged out of an actual pleasant present moment into the theoretical, Darwinian future. It was crazy. He was not a real young man anyway. He was an anomaly, a Frankenstein monster or hotrod human, with some parts old and some parts souped up, the whole contraption unbalanced and unstable.

He heard Lilly in the hall, knocking softly at the door to

the room he was supposed to be in.

"Ben?" she said, "Ben, I need you."

He slipped out of bed, cracked the door to Louise's room, and stuck his head out.

"Over here," he said, "What's wrong?"

"I'm bleeding." She was cupping the crotch of her pajamas.

"Just a minute."

Ben hurried into his clothes. He slipped out of the door and took Lilly down the hall to the living room.

"What happened?"

"Blood, down there. I think I got my... you know, period." She looked down and seemed very small. Ben put his arm around her thin shoulders. She felt like a bird.

"It's going to be okay," Ben said.

"What's going on?" Louise said from the hall. She flipped on the light.

Ben winced at the sudden brightness. "Lilly needs some help. Do you have any, um, feminine hygiene stuff?"

"Not anymore. Not for a couple years now. I thought you knew."

Ben said to Lilly, "I'll have to go to the store. I'll be right back."

"Take me with you."

"Wouldn't you rather stay here with Louise?"

"No, take me with you."

Louise took her keys from the kitchen counter and handed them to Ben.

"Take my car," she said. "I'm going back to bed."

In the car on the way to the 24-hour store, Lilly asked, "Was your wife mad at me?"

"No, not at all. She was just surprised. Mad at me maybe."

"Are you getting back together with her?"

"No."

"But you were in her bedroom."

"I know. It's complicated."

She was quiet for a while. They pulled into the Quickie Mart parking lot.

"Adults say that a lot," she said.

"What?"

"'It's complicated.'"

"Well, it is complicated."

"Sure, but that doesn't explain anything. Everything's complicated."

"Wait here, I'll be right back."

The store was too brightly lit, the music too lively and loud for four o'clock in the morning. Ben was dreading this particular consumer experience. At least the person behind the counter was a woman, so she'd know something. But she was pretty old, so maybe she wasn't up to speed on the latest feminine products.

"Excuse me," he said, "I need some help getting something for my daughter." He held his hands out, as if cupping a box of a specific size, just couldn't remember the brand name. "She got her first period tonight and we didn't have any... I mean, we weren't... prepared with..."

"Oh, that's so cute," the woman said. "Caught you completely by surprise, didn't it?"

"I guess so."

"Relax, sweetie, we got just what you need."

She came out from behind the counter and led him down an aisle to some crowded shelves.

"All our girl stuff is right here," she said, "between the condoms and the corn nuts." She chuckled and handed him an antiseptic white box branded in calming blue and healthy green.

"Okay, first you gotta get these thin pads, they're probably what she needs right now." She handed him another, thicker box. "But get these thicker ones too, just in case her flow is heavy." She gave him a thinner, longer package. "And get these. They're tampons and they go inside, which might freak her out at first, but they're best for nighttime."

She led him back to the counter. Ben set the boxes down and got out his wallet. The woman pulled a single red rose from a bucket on the counter.

"Better get her this too." She said, putting the flower on top of all the boxes.

"A rose?" Ben said.

"It's a symbol, honey. You're little girl's a woman now — it's a big deal."

"What if she has questions? How do I..."

"Instructions in the boxes, more on the net. She'll be fine." She handed him his change.

"Thank you so much." He paid and scurried out to the car.

When they got home Lilly retreated to the bathroom with the boxes and her handheld. She emerged with a shy smile on her face.

"It's all right now," she said.

Ben handed her a cup of tea and the rose.

"This is for you," he said. "The oracle of the Quickie Mart said you're officially a woman now, and it's a big deal."

She didn't say anything right away. Just took the tea and sipped it, looking at her rose. When the tea was almost gone, she said, "Thank you for helping me."

"It was my honor," Ben said. "How do you feel?"

"I think I feel like Herbie Too, when Sixsmith's signature tune was golden, and their drummer's number was platinum at the same time. Remember?"

Ben shrugged, unwilling to admit ignorance of yet another universally recognized band. "So you feel, what? Happy? Surprised? Worried?"

She just smiled. "It's complicated."

43. Fleas

"You have to understand," the cop said. "I'm fraud squad, not homicide. There's nothing I can do about a Malaysian break-in gone wrong. The Malays say that's all it was, and Interpol's not interested. They won't touch it. Not unless there's some new evidence. Have you got any?"

"No, not really," Ben said. "But it's part of a bigger pattern: They manipulated the human trials. They cheated me out of my bonuses. They are downplaying some serious side effects that could hurt thousands of people, maybe millions."

"That's not fraud, that's business as usual."

Ben just stared at him.

"Sorry," the cop said, "Bad joke. A little too… cynical, I guess. But you see my point?"

"It happens every day, so it's okay?"

"No, it's not okay, but it's part of the world we live in. Look around you."

He spread his hands and nearly touched the opposite walls. They were in a cubical in the basement. It was so close to the parking garage Ben could hear the chargers humming.

The cop rapped on his desk. "San Francisco has one of the most effective consumer fraud departments in the country, and it's me and two other guys. Our squad is really Public Relations, with handcuffs. If a fortune teller bilks your granny out of all the UN bucks in her teapot, I'm your guy. But forget corporate fraud. Corporations are the new nations. I'm just the sheriff of Tiny Town."

"Then I'm wasting my time here," Ben said. He got up to leave.

"Sorry I couldn't be more help. You and I are like the fleas on the rhino's butt. Kalimer is a big rhino, they won't even notice our bite."

On the ferry back to Santa Rosa, Ben picked at the scabs on his neck and stared out the window at the gray water. His restless leg was jumping up an down like a snare drummer, little migraine flashes of light in his vision flaring up with each down-beat, and his oncoming headache about to burst into throbbing song. He felt vast and without boundaries, spread thin as gas across the universe with no way to pull himself together. At the same time he felt very small, a microscopic flyspeck on Kalimer's windshield, a flea on a rhino.

Kalimer and the other drug empires were just too big. GE and Toyota were too big. QED and Google and Fireside were too big. It was the theme of Ben's life—giving over his autonomy and power to a company, and then not being able to reclaim it and get it back. He had traded freedom and truth for security and lies and he couldn't back out of the deal.

44. Monk on Fire

Things went better for Ben and Lilly on their second visit to Aunt Sylvia. They showed up with lunch in sacks and a file of pictures of Glory in Australia and Malaysia. They linked up three ways and went over the photos, sitting hip to haunch on a couch so they could all see Lilly's handheld. In ten minutes the link and memories of Glory had them laughing together and finishing each other's sentences.

Lilly pointed to a glowing orange abstraction. "That's our tent at sunset. The sun used to hit it just for a few minutes at the end of the day, in the winter. She always used to tell a story at night and rub my back when I was falling asleep. She'd say what the characters were saying in this funny voice–always the same funny voice for all the characters. She really sucked at voices."

"I know," Sylvia said, "When we were girls in Perth,

she'd sing pop songs and they all sounded the same. She couldn't carry a tune at all..."

"...but she loved to sing anyway," Ben said. "That's what I loved about her--she wasn't self-conscious like most people. She really knew how to be herself, and she shared herself with you, without reservation."

"I'm sorry I was so snotty when you were here last time," Sylvia said.

"No problem. You were upset. It's a hard time for all of us." Ben patted her hand. He felt some ridges on her forearm and absently traced them with his fingertip. They were smart tattoos. Usually Ben didn't care for them. He thought that smart tattoos trivialized genetic engineering–kids tinkering with their genomes just so their skin cells would express melanin in a design and thicken into fake scarification patterns. When it was done poorly at some underground scar parlor, they ended up with resistant infections or recurring skin cancers that were difficult to shut down. Some of the results were impressive, though, like Sylvia's tribal runes spiraling around her arm.

Lilly removed her link and asked Sylvia, "Can I use your desktop?"

"Sure, hon. There's some games on there. I think I've got Rendition."

"Green. Thanks." Lilly trotted off to the work area at the back of the space, leaving Ben and Sylvia alone on the couch, in the deepening connection afforded by their linking.

Ben's mind had wandered a little. He couldn't quite remember if he had said all that stuff about scar parlors out loud, or if he had just thought it to himself, or if maybe even Sylvia had said it. Was that the Rejuven or the link?

Sylvia was still sitting close to him, their hips touching, though Lilly had left room for her to move away. Still linked, they didn't want to separate. Sylvia took his hand and rubbed his knuckles. To Ben it seemed like all the nerves in his body were concentrated in his hand and all his attention was on the electric tingle of her touch.

She was saying, "Lilly is a great kid. She really likes you. She looks at you like some kind of hero."

"No, she's my hero."

"I wanted to ask you. Lilly told me on the phone you're taking some kind of wonder drug that makes you younger. What's that about?"

"It's called Rejuven. It makes some things in your body younger, or makes them feel younger."

"How is that possible?"

"Rejuven cranks up your metabolism and stimulates hormones and endorphins. There's some evidence that it actually makes your cells divide more efficiently and more times, which means you live longer."

"That sounds great. Where can I get some?" She gave his hand an extra squeeze.

"It's not all good news."

"What do you mean?"

"There are subtle side effects. Rejuven is kind of addictive. It makes you feel young and alive in an artificial way, like alcohol or cocaine. It's like overclocking a computer, or rechipping your car for performance at all costs, regardless of reliability or longevity. If you give into all the urges to stay up late, party and drink and dance and screw, well then you undo all the good work the drug is doing at the cellular level—you wear yourself out, burn brighter, but for the same amount of time, or even less time."

"Like burning the candle at both ends?"

"Yeah. It's like Rejuven makes the candle longer, but you burn it at both ends. Or it makes the candle longer but adds kerosene to the wax so that it burns faster and lasts exactly as long as the shorter, original candle."

"Still, it sounds pretty exciting."

"There are some other side effects. Rapid mood cycles. Up one day, down the next. Anger, depression. Sometimes I think all I've done is find a really complicated way to induce bipolar disease. I think I may have unleashed more trouble on the world than help."

"What do you mean?" She released his hand and turned to face him more directly.

"Some thinkers say that there's an optimum number of years that humans can live, given the level of civilization at the time, how much the culture has evolved and supports wellbeing. In the stone age it was thirty years. It was thirty years for millions of years. Eventually we figured out agriculture and it was forty years, for quite a while, up through the middle ages. In Victorian England it was sixty years. By 2000 it was eighty years. Now it's a hundred years. With Rejuven and whatever comes after, it might hit 125 years before I die. The curve looks exponential so far."

"Like rising faster and faster?"

"Exactly, in a sharp hockey stick curve. Some say it leads to a singularity of immortality. We'll figure out how to merge with computers, become immortal artificial intelligences, or something. You and I won't live long enough to see that."

Sylvia fixed him with an unblinking stare, looking right through him, beyond him, far off to some intuitive realm not available to mere mortals like Ben Rasmussen. She shut her eyes briefly, then opened them and she was back with him.

"I don't care to live that long," she said. All that sci fi robot stuff doesn't sound like much fun." She slapped her thigh. "I like my meat."

Ben slapped her thigh as well. It felt firm and strong. "Me too. But I'd give up my meat if it meant living forever." Realistically, Ben suspected that the flesh and the mind could only be sustained so far. He thought that somewhere between 100 and 200 years, there was a limit. Or should be. Beyond the limit, if we can go there at all, we are no longer human.

"The idea of living forever scares me," Sylvia said. "It just sounds so long. How could I continue doing art? All my ideas would get used up eventually, and there'd be nothing left."

"Glory told me you were a famous artist. What kind of art do you do?"

"It's web-based performance art. Satire. But it's made me more infamous than famous. What I do is make fake video feeds and websites and webinars and forums and stuff, purportedly from some big corpse like Realaize or Google or Microsoft. They look official at first glance, with all the correct logos and mission statements and ads. Then the deeper you go, the twistier and kinkier and funnier and eviler they get. I have had to keep a very low profile about my actual identity and where I live and all."

"Is that why you sent us encrypted coordinates instead of an address?"

"Partly, yes. I need to stay in the shadows, like that old hacker gal, Anonymous, who recruited other nerds to do the really dirty work. She never got caught until she was like fifty years old. Of course, things were looser back then. It's getting harder and harder to do what I do, to stay ahead of the zombie bots, to get enough safe donations. Corps keep hacking my accounts and drop boxes and cutouts, so I have to keep changing things all the time. It gets exhausting."

"Would you say you're a hacker, then?"

"No, I'm not a hacker. More of a mimic, an impressionist, a digital court fool. I don't try to hack the big sites. I stay on the surface and just mimic them. I don't really know how to subvert their security. I just put the appearance of security on my sites, but they really have little protection. That's why they don't last, why it's a performance art–because it is almost as time-limited as monk setting herself on fire on the sidewalk. You have to be there to see it in person. If you hear about a little late, it's over. The live site is gone, and the archive sites slowly fade away."

45. A Story with Teeth

"You have to understand," the reporter on Ben's screen said. "There's not much I can do with this story."

"Let's pretend I don't understand," Ben said. "You explain it to me."

"There are proprietary information laws that prevent me from using what you've got about the drug trials. I'd love to write 'Kalimer Fakes Rejuven Results,' but I can't do it on your say-so alone. That's one problem. If I write about your demotion and firing: 'Kalimer Cans Inconvenient Scientist,' and the story has any teeth in it, we'll both be sued for slandering and defaming a corporate person."

"That's ridiculous."

"I know, but that's life in the Corpocracy. You're the disgruntled employee in the tower with a rifle, and I'm the aider and abettor who gave you the key to the tower. It's not worth the risk to me."

"The way this is going, nobody's going to accuse you of aiding me."

"Very funny. But that's exactly right. You're too hot to handle. You're a corporate citizen without a country. Kalimer has revoked your passport. What you've got left is 'Waivered Kalimer Scientist's Girlfriend Killed in Kuala Lumpur.' Not much of a story without the Rejuven angle. Almost sounds like you did it. If you'd like to confess, I could report that."

Ben just stared at her. Everybody was a comedienne.

"Sorry," she said. "Bad joke. The only thing I can suggest is trying to get this story in the back door, as part of a technical article in some scientific journal. Can you write some of this stuff up as a science paper?"

"No, I already thought of that. None of the journals will accept any papers from the corporately disaffected. They're all funded by industry in one way or another. It's more political than an African satrapy."

Ben hung up. His leg was vibrating again. He was having more of his "growing younger pains." His mind was restless and it was hard to follow one line of thought very far. He took a couple anti-spasmodics and washed them down with a beer. How had he got in this situation? It made him so angry that people could steal his ideas, pervert them into something that makes money, and then not give him any.

He originally went into research to help people, to make their lives better. At least he thought that was his motivation, mostly. But years among the greedy and the thieving had made sticking to your ideals so hard. Eventually it was mostly about the money, the houses, the cars, and the planes. But he still wanted to help people, in his spare time, when he could. Now when he was trying to tell his story, trying to make a difference, he was frustrated at every turn. He felt as powerless as the adolescent he had become.

46. For Me to Know

Ben and Lilly were spending more and more time at Sylvia's place. Lilly had her sleeping bag stashed behind the couch and Ben had set up a cot in the corner.

Ben was looking over Lilly's shoulder, watching her play at geopolitics in her ongoing Rendition game.

"You could call the new country Rapscallia," Ben said, "because it was founded by rascals and scalliwags."

She winced. "That's too Huckleberry Finn. Nobody reads that anymore, except you and me."

"So what? It's your world. You can name the countries anything you want."

"Precisely, Dr. Rasmussen. Anything *I* want."

"What are you going to call it then?"

"I was thinking Bendoverstan. Or Rasmussia."

"Okay, okay. I'll leave you alone." He ruffled her hair. "It's getting late, though. Don't forget to go to bed."

He went around the corner into the kitchen area. Sylvia was perched on a stool, bent over her own handheld.

"Look at this, Ben," she said, turning the screen so he could see. She dragged the video bug back a ways. Ben leaned in so he could hear the tinny sound. Her hair smelled like lemons and he could feel the warmth of her skin rising to caress his cheek.

It was the latest episode of the InMates-L program. Kalimer had been pushing the Rejuven plotline heavily for the past four segments.

The fifty-year-old Haunch character came out of solitary looking like a thirty-five-year-old who had been at a makeover spa for a month. She strutted and preened in front of her rival, Boobs.

"I feel as young as I look," she said. "Those pills are magic."

"Where did you get them?" Boobs asked. "You never got the shots, and you ain't in the pill program."

"That's for me to know and you to shut the fuck up."

The obvious implication was that her stolen stash of Rejuven capsules had worked perfectly, without her receiving any of the injections or medical monitoring that the members of the regular human trial had been receiving.

Ben rested his hand lightly on Sylvias shoulder. The hand was trembling slightly, partly desire, partly the Rejuven. She leaned into him.

Ben said, "Kalimer is really touting their single capsule formulation, building demand prior to product launch."

"They must be pretty close to approval for sale, huh?"

"Yeah. We'll start seeing regular ads for Rejuven soon. When we do, I'd say they're sixty days from commercial release."

He glanced toward the alcove where Lilly was spreading her sleeping bag on the couch. She could hear them but not see them, so he stole a quick kiss.

"How's that cot?" Sylvia asked. "Pretty comfortable?"

"It's fine, till something better comes along."

She put a finger on his lips. "Soon."

47. Beefy Guys

Ben reached inside his jacket and felt the miniature battery-operated bullhorn. He was standing against a wall in the large conference hall at Kalimer headquarters, as close as he could get to the stage where Trujib Kapoor was about to announce the official release of Rejuven. Kalimer's press conference was a throwback to an earlier age when investment bankers, product managers, and presidents of the United States would call an actual in-the-flesh meeting to announce some big news such as a merger of former rivals, a declaration of war or a new flavor of breakfast cereal.

The audience was packed with business reporters and their camera crews. There were even a couple of camera drones whirring near the ceiling, angling for a dramatic shot of the podium, where Trujib Kapoor stood resplendent in a silvery gray overvest that clashed with the dominant orange tone of his complexion. Like a preacher describing the horrors of hell, Trujib was waxing eloquent about the horrors of aging.

"...tragic that our brightest inventors, mathematicians, and CEOs tend to peak at age thirty-two and experience a swift decline of powers, hostage to their own senescence."

Ben waited against the wall, bouncing a little, up on his toes and down again, fingering the bullhorn in his jacket. Trujib finished his litany of aging symptoms and embarked on a recap of the history of anti-aging pharmacology. Ben mentally

163

rehearsed his ringing denunciation of Kalimer, Trujib, and Rejuven. His main points blazed in his mind in a fiery all caps font. He felt full of power and righteous rage. With all these reporters in the audience, his side of the story would finally be heard. They couldn't ignore this. He waited impatiently until he sensed that Trujib was about to start talking about Rejuven, then pulled out the bullhorn and took a deep breath.

Suddenly there were two beefy guys in dark vests on either side of Ben. Their hands clamped onto his forearms and pulled the bullhorn from his lips. The bullhorn was twisted from his grasp and one arm was swung around behind his back. Pain flared in his elbow and shoulder.

"You don't want to do that, sir," one side of beef said, giving Ben's arm a tug behind his back.

"You'll need to come with us, sir," the other side of beef said.

He took Ben by the hand and pulling him toward the exit. He had Ben's free hand in some kind of painful come along grip that was only tolerable if Ben kept up with him. Ben started to shout out in protest, but they hustled him out the back door before many in the audience were even aware of a disruption.

"You can't do this," Ben shouted, but they ignored him. They dragged him into a service elevator and the three of them rode down to Corporate Security in the basement. At no time did side of beef number one relax his hold on Ben. All of Ben's new muscle strength in his newly young body was nothing compared to two genuine young tough guys who knew their business.

They pushed him into a nicely appointed office where Darius Jones was waiting behind a real wood desk. The beefs sat Ben down in a visitors chair, gently placed his bullhorn on Jones' desk, and left, closing the door behind them.

"Doctor Rasmussen," the Security Chief said, "What are we going to do with you?"

Ben sat in the visitor's chair, rubbing his sore hand, glaring at Jones. This was the man who had killed Glory.

Jones shook his head slowly, a more-in-sadness-than-in-anger gesture. "Did you really think you could try to spread all that crap about Kalimer on the net, and show up here with fake press ID and a bullhorn, of all things? Did you really think we wouldn't notice? Wouldn't do something about it?"

Ben just stared at him.

"Oh, so now you have nothing say? Now, when you should be begging me not to turn you over to the cops, not to ruin your life? Fine. Listen then, because you're not getting the message. First you were waivered to ChemGen in Malaysia because you weren't a team player. But you didn't get the message. Instead of knuckling down and earning your way back into our good graces, you stole proprietary materials and information and made groundless threats. So you were terminated, but you still didn't get the message."

"You sent someone to search my apartment," Ben said, "And they killed my friend. I got that message loud and clear. You're going to pay for that."

"You see, this is what I mean. You're bankrupt, divorced, disgraced, discredited. And still you don't get the message. Here's the short version: you can't win. Nobody is going to believe your paranoid fantasies. Not about the evils of Kalimer and Rejuven. Not about some dead blond in Kuala Lumpur."

"I'm not paranoid, and they're not fantasies. You can't keep me quiet forever. I'm going to expose you eventually."

Jones smiled sadly and said something into his phone that Ben couldn't make out. "I'm sorry to hear you say that."

One of the sides of beef came in, leading Lilly by the hand. Her face was streaked from crying.

"Lilly!" Ben said, "Are you okay?"

"These men said you're in trouble. Are you okay?

"Sure sweetie. I'm fine." Ben hugged Lilly, pulling her next to him.

He asked Jones, "What the hell is going on here?"

"We've invited Ms. Banks here to escort you home," Jones said. "We were worried you might hurt yourself, or someone else. And we didn't want to call the cops." Jones indicated for Lilly to sit in the corner, to Ben's left.

"Before you leave, I want to make one point." Jones opened his desk drawer and took out a large gray handgun, a revolver that looked ancient and heavy. He put it on the desk with the barrel pointing toward Ben.

"We're very worried about you," Jones said, "Not because of the threats you have made, but because you were a valuable member of the Kalimer family, and we don't forget things like that."

"Very cute," Ben said, forcing himself to keep his voice low and quiet. "The fake concern, the veiled threats. Bringing Lilly here is kidnapping, plain and simple. The gun makes it a threat of violence, makes it extortion."

"Gun?" Jones said, probably for the benefit of any recording device Ben might have, "I have no gun. This is a paperweight. An ornament." He reached out and rotated the pistol so that the barrel was pointing at Lilly.

"What you don't understand," he continued, "is that your behavior is not just unwise. It has consequences. For yourself, and for others, especially those you love, who are in your care."

Jones leaned back in his chair and looked at Lilly, then back to Ben. It was a clear threat without actually saying anything incriminating, and it was the opening Ben had been waiting for.

Jones had made a fatal mistake. He thought he was dealing with an old scientist in his sixties, with sixty-year-old reflexes and an intact set of cautious instincts. But no. Inside at least, Ben was now twenty—invulnerable, impulsive, prone to action without considering the consequences. So when Jones placed the gun on his desk, trying to be cute by letting it lie there, not picking it up and pointing it at Ben, Ben knew at once that he could grab it and use it. The sixty-year-old scientist made note of the safety lever and the dull gleam of bullets in the chambers. The twenty-year-old desperado figured the angles, sprang out of the chair, and grabbed the gun. The scientist backed against the wall, flipped the safety lever and took careful aim. When Jones lunged at Ben over the desk, the desperado shot him.

BANG! The report was louder than TV. The kickback was literally like his hand had been kicked. The room filled up with blue smoke that stung the eyes. Lilly was out of her chair, crying and clinging to his shoulder. Jones was on the floor behind the desk.

The door burst open and the two sides of beef rushed in. Ben was behind the door and had the drop on them. His desperado wanted to kill them too, but his scientist just shot one in the foot.

He said to the other beef, "Get us out of the building and I won't shoot you. Do it now." He thumbed back the hammer.

The beef led them through several corridors, into the parking garage, and to Ben's car. Ben took the beef's phone and handheld and anything electronic that looked like it could make a call. He told him, "Now leave us," and the beef disappeared. Ben and Lilly drove out of the garage, breaking off the plastic barrier arm thing at the gate, just like the movies. It didn't make much of a noise or do much damage. It seemed designed to break. People must do it all the time. Ben's wondered that he had time to think about such a mundane thing, but time seemed to be slowed down, and he had lots of time to consider every angle of every second.

48. Bona Fides

Being on the run was a drug. It changed everything, put a new complexion on the world, made every detail in Ben's environment stand out, separate and unique. He and Lilly were in a spotlight at the center of the universe. Fear wasn't quite the word. He was afraid, yes. Lilly was afraid for sure. But he was also exhilarated, turned on. Each moment held extra significance. He existed in a be-here-now kind of Zen bubble, a bad guy state of grace.

And then just when he was feeling like the hero of his own action movie, the memory of shooting Jones would flash across his mind and he'd start shaking inside. He'd feel a deep tremor of guilt, a groundswell of shame, a sinkhole of dread. He'd get tunnel vision, palpitations, clammy palms. He felt like he had plummeted off a cliff and was in free fall, about to smash into the ground.

Ben had to hold it together for Lilly's sake. At Louise's house in Santa Rosa they packed two small bags. He figured they had maybe an hour or two before Kalimer called in the cops and they showed up at Louise's front door. He threw socks and underwear and shirts into a gym bag and called out to Lilly: "Don't' forget your inhaler."

"Don't do this," Louise said. She had been following him around the house, actually wringing her hands like a heroine in a melodrama. "If you won't turn yourself in, at least leave Lilly here with me."

"I can't take that chance. They took her right off your front porch like an old newspaper. You don't know these people. They'll do anything to neutralize me, including hurting Lilly. She's safer with me."

"But the cops will protect her."

"I can't count on that. The cops will protect Kalimer and their shareholders, same as usual."

"What am I going to tell the cops if they show up here?"

"The truth." Ben tossed in his remaining Rejuven and zipped up the bag. "We were here, we stole your car, and you don't know where we're going."

They drove north in Louise's runabout, taking surface streets with lots of stoplights, so the cameras could see their car. They abandoned the car in a Rapid Transit parking lot and boarded a local train headed further north to Eureka on the Oregon border. On the train they went car-to-car until they found one with a spray-painted camera.

"Put on all the clothes you brought," Ben said, "make yourself look fatter."

"I wouldn't do this for anybody but you."

"I appreciate it. Put your hoodie on top and cover your head."

Ben pulled one of Louise dresses over his jeans and T shirt. He clapped one of her wigs on his head and Lilly laughed.

"Oh Ben, you are such an ugly woman."

"Shhh. Slump down and walk slowly. We're getting off at the next stop."

They got off at Cloverdale and crossed to the southbound platform. They were in luck. A train was just about to pull out, and the car they boarded had a broken camera.

After changing clothes and trains three times, they arrived finally at Sylvia's storefront in the Maul. Sylvia let them in and stared at them in amazement.

"I didn't know I was having a costume party."

"It's no party," Ben said. He slumped onto the couch and explained what had happened—the killing, how they had escaped, and so on.

"The cops will probably look here eventually," he said, "but not for a while. We can stay the night and move on."

Sylvia gave him what he had come to call her X-ray Stare, the direct, eyeball to eyeball scrutiny with which she gazed at you and through you at the same time. As he expected, she closed her eyes briefly, made a decision, opened her eyes and made her pronouncement.

"You'd better not stay in my place," Sylvia said, "in case the cops get here faster than you think. We should find you a squat."

"A what?"

"Not everybody here in the Maul is on the books. Haven't you ever seen Squat & Gardens or any of the other squatter sites?"

Patrick Fanning

"I guess not. What are squatter sites?"

"Online magazines that tell you how to take over abandoned retail space with your gang, hijack power and water, run generators, barricade most entrances, where to poop, how to get in and out without being spotted."

"But I don't have a gang."

"Sure you do. You've got me and Lilly. Doesn't he, girl?"

Lilly and Sylvia bumped fists.

"Or you might find a nice foreclosed house." Sylvia continued. "That's a big thing too. Not all the malls are organized like this one and used for subsidized housing. There's a lot of unsubsidized space you can get into."

"How do you know all this?"

"I squatted for years before I lucked into this place. Come along, we'll ask Roger."

The three of them went into the parking lot of the mall. At a card table under an awning hung off an old trailer up on blocks, she introduced him to Roger. He was a skinny guy in a caftan, with tattoos crawling up his neck like spiders.

Sylvia said, "I need a quiet place for my cousin to hang out for few days. What you got?"

Roger poked at his phone and muttered, "Dry cleaners other side of 101, a little smelly. Boiler room in condemned apartment building, juice still on. Cubicles in an old grocery on Pine."

"Anything nearby?"

"House sitting situation, three blocks away. Water from a hose, propane camp stove. He'd have to feed the cat and water the plants."

"Sounds perfect. How long?"

"Tenant's staying with the county, got about two more months on his sentence. Your cousin got references?"

"I'll vouch for him."

"Okay."

They checked out the house-sit. It was actually a converted single car garage, behind a burned-out house. They entered through an artfully distressed lean-to shed that hid a new steel door cut into the side of the garage. Inside it was furnished with thrift store bargains and new camping gear. Water came from a hose dripping into a sump in the corner. There was a bucket next to the toilet for flushing, and power from an extension cord that snaked under the fence and into the guts of the rear neighbor's hot tub. There was a camp stove for cooking and a newish sleeping bag on an old mattress. No windows, and the old garage door covered over with black plastic garbage bags and duct tape to keep the light and warmth from escaping. A couple of small ventilation holes punched through the walls, high up under the eaves to keep the rain out.

"All the comforts of home," Sylvia said. "You'll be safe here."

"It's like camping," Lilly said, kneeling on the mattress and petting an old orange cat that had followed them in.

"Thanks," Ben said. "This will do nicely." He squeezed Sylvia's hand and gave her a one-armed hug.

Sylvia squeezed back, holding the pressure while she gave him her intense, direct, basilisk stare. And with that, Ben knew that he had passed some final threshold, that he and Sylvia were now lovers, although they had still not done the deed. Perhaps being on the run gave him new bona fides that he never had as a straight scientist or mere boyfriend of her late sister. Now that he was on the lam, he was an outsider like her, so she could fully accept him. Or maybe she was finally seeing how much Lilly trusted him, loved him even, and that melted the last measure of reserve.

49. Huck and Jim

"You stay here," Sylvia said to Ben. "Lilly and I will go back, and I'll tell Roger you'll take the place."

"I want to stay here with Ben," Lilly said.

Ben hugged Lilly, "Okay. We'll be fine here." To Sylvia he said, "See you tomorrow." Sylvia hugged both of them together, a little awkwardly, and left.

Lilly lay on the mattress, petting the cat. Ben alongside, petting Lilly's shoulder. Lilly fell fast asleep. She was worn out by the traumatic events and feelings of the day—being told that Ben was in trouble, being taken by Jones' men to San Francisco, seeing Ben argue with and then shoot Jones, then the dramatic escape from the parking garage, all the costume changes and doubling back on the trains.

Ben drifted into sleep himself. He dreamed a long series of disconnected scenes of being questioned by officious dark figures, of not knowing the right answers, of looking for something he couldn't find or even quite remember. Half asleep, he relived the encounter with Jones, thinking "This time I must not shoot him. I've got to do something else." But every time he did shoot him, did grab the gun and blast away, did jump off that cliff.

He woke up to Lilly crying and hiccupping next to him, reaching out for him. She had had a nightmare. He held her and rubbed her back.

"It's okay," he said. "it was just a dream. It's not real."

"There was a lion, and a wolf, and a dead dog."

"It's okay. Try to go back to sleep."

"I can't. I need you to read to me."

Ben took out his handheld. The home screen looked funny till he remembered that Sylvia had made him turn off several functions and remove some apps that might give away his location to the cops. But he could still read books. He opened Huckleberry Finn. They were at the part where Huck and the escaped slave Jim are hiding on an island, watching a steamboat full of people who are searching for Huck's supposedly drowned body.

Ben started to read but Lilly interrupted him.

"Link, please." She handed him his link and put hers on. Ben slipped the plastic halo around his ears. His ears and temples were rashy and sore. He had been breaking out with little pimples in odd places. The skin around his eyes felt clammy and weird. He hoped he wasn't getting another migraine.
"Ben, you awake?"
"Sure. Sorry, I guess I faded out on you again." He sat up with his back against the wall, and Lilly laid down with her head in his lap.

As he read, Ben felt the tension seep out of him. His voice slowed and deepened. He enjoyed reading to Lilly while linked, but as she got sleepy and fell asleep, he got drowsy too. Some nights they only made it through a couple of paragraphs.

He was disoriented when he woke up. The garage apartment had no natural light, so he had no idea if it was still dark or broad day. He turned on his handheld and checked the news.

Kalimer Pharmaceuticals announced today the final approval of its long-awaited anti-aging drug Rejuven. The geriagenic agents in Rejuven have been shown to reverse the apparent, cellular, and genetic effects of aging, increasing lifespan by a factor of eight to fourteen percent. Or as Li'l Piece on InMates says, "you looks and feels like a punk again."

In a related story, Kalimer Security Chief Darius Jones the third was shot and killed during the Rejuven press conference. Police are seeking Ben Rasmussen, former Kalimer contractee, in connection with the shooting.

Ben's own face stared up at him from his screen, a photo from company files, looking sixtyish and old. He looked more like thirty-five or forty now, leaner and meaner. No one would identify him from the old photo.

His image on the screen blurred out of focus and he had to blink and rub his eyes. Another possible side effect to lay at Rejuven's door. His crotch and the insides of his thighs were itching and he scratched them quietly, trying not to wake Lilly. He felt jumpy and scared, wide awake and no longer sleepy. Was this feeling a natural reaction to the situation, or another side effect of the drug? Now that Rejuven was headed to market, would he continue taking it?

He loved looking and feeling younger, but the price was high. He wondered why he was always rushing and straining to live longer and be younger. It was a persistent greediness for life that had informed all his choices of school and career and research focus. But in the push toward the long future, he tended to lose the present. He often didn't experience what was right in front of him, right here and now in the present moment. He felt vaguely guilty and stupid. Instead of living fully and deeply the span allotted him, he was skimming over more time than was his fair share, not really living at all, most days. He needed an alien sidekick like Yoda, whispering in his ear once in a while: "Live deep you must, Live in the now you must."

He lay there listening to the girl's breathing. Lilly had made much of this clearer to Ben. During all their crazy time together, no matter how busy or on the run, she insisted on reading aloud together before bedtime, with their links on. It made the stories more intense, more a shared excitement, laughing and crying at all the same places. It didn't really matter what they read—some old romance novel on Glory's 'vice, or the horoscope, or the agony aunt letters on the advice websites. Huck Finn was great. Lilly said, "I always see me as Huck and you as Jim."

"No, I'm Huck."

"No, me." And they'd laugh.

50. That Antsy Feeling

In the morning there was a knock on the door and Sylvia yelled, " Open up. It's Sylvia."

She came in bearing coffee and orange juice and sweet rolls. They sat on the mattress and had brunch while she filled them in.

"No cops yet, but it's just a matter of time. They'll back-track your movements over the last few weeks and come down here, just to see."

"The photo of me on line doesn't really look like me." He was restless. He got up and started pacing back and forth.

"They'll fix that. I'm sure they have you on camera from yesterday."

"We can't stay around here. We should go to Mexico or something."

"That won't help. Mexico just signed that extradition treaty with IMF. Anybody Kalimer wants, Mexico will give up. Might as well stay here. Anyway, you can't drag Lilly to Mexico."

"He's not dumping me here," Lilly said. "Anywhere Ben goes, I go."

Sylvia sighed. "Life on the run is no place for a kid." Her handheld chimed and she studied the screen. "The cops are at my place. They'll ask around, probably find someone who saw you here yesterday. I'll tell them you came, borrowed some cash, and took off. That will hold them for a while."

"You're going to tell them we were here?" Lilly asked. "Don't do that."

"No," Ben said, "That's smart. Sylvia shouldn't tell them any lies they can check up on. What about Roger, can we trust him?"

"I think so. For a while. But we have to talk about what

you're going to do in the long run. I think you two should split up now, and leave Lilly with me. I can go back to my place with her stuff, and say you dropped her here on your way to Mexico or someplace. You don't want to be on the run with a kid."

Lilly glared at her. "I won't be any trouble. I can go with Ben and be like his daughter and stuff."

Ben put his arm around her shoulder and said to Sylvia, "If Lilly wants to come, I want her with me. I'll look less like a man on the run with my adorable little daughter along."

Lilly wriggled out from under the arm. "Yuck."

"Whatever," Sylvia said. "You say that now, but how long can you keep it up? They won't stop looking for you as long as you're alive."

"Maybe that's the answer. Fake my death."

"Sure, you've already faked your youth. You're juking and jiving like a teenager."

"Very funny." Ben became aware that he had been pacing around the tiny space, back and forth, burning up the extra, insistent energy that screamed inside him like a runaway generator.

"Sit down," Sylvia said. "We need to really talk this through."

Ben sat across from her on the mattress.

"Put this on," Sylvia said, holding out his link set.

"Sure, I guess." He took it and put it on.

"If we're going to talk about this, I need to know that you're not lying to me. The link will help."

"Sure, okay, glad to do it." Ben settled the link around his ears and tried to look honest and harmless.

Sylvia laughed. "You're blushing. Just relax. I cannot tolerate phony people. That's what I love about the link."

"Isn't it awkward to ask everybody you meet to link up, and kind of...artificial?"

"I don't ask everyone. Just when it's important. And yes, it's artificial in one way. It's artificially enhancing feelings. But at least it's based in authenticity. It's almost impossible to lie

176

once you're linked deeply."

"Impossible? Really?"

"Well, not impossible, but very obvious. When I'm linked to a liar, I feel incredibly antsy and unbalanced, like I'm on speed. It's unmistakable.

"I think that's why they never link in the corporate world–they lie constantly. Being phony is a job requirement. You have to stifle what you really think and try to appear to think only along company lines. You have to root for the home team constantly, even when you see it losing and making you lose, dragging you down with it."

"I don't see how you can live like that."

"I can't. I can no longer tolerate my own hypocrisy, my own collusion in the Big Lie. There are so many big lies."

"I know. Like Global Cooling."

"Right. And terrorism."

"Consumer confidence."

"Enlightened Self-Interest." They laughed.

Lilly put down the book she was pretending to read. "You guys are silly," she said. "I thought you were going to talk about the cops. We are fugitives, you know."

"Relax," Sylvia said. "We're just syncing our links. This guy's a natural." She poked Ben's knee. Lilly sniffed and returned to her book.

Sylvia said, "What's the deal with this drug? You're like an early adopter? Testing it before all the side effects are known?"

"That's right. I'm an early adopter. Sometimes the big drug companies do it this way: have real people try it in the real world."

"So you're ahead of the curve?"

"I'm so far ahead of the curve, I'm on a straight line. So far ahead of the wave, I'm on the beach already."

"I have to admit, it makes you look younger. But it also makes you act younger. Or are you really this jumpy?"

"I can handle it. I'm going to taper off pretty soon, anyway. Probably."

"I'm getting that antsy feeling. You're lying to me. Or maybe to yourself."

Ben took off his link. "I'm getting a killer headache. Can we talk about this later?" He got up an resumed his pacing, holding his head and massaging his temples as if he could dig his fingers into his skull and crush the pain.

51. A Dreadful Attraction

Sylvia left in frustration, nothing settled. Ben guessed that this would not be the day they consummated their new relationship. He laid down on the mattress. His head was throbbing and his vision blurring and flaring in little bursts of light. He seemed to hear a high-pitched squeal that disappeared as soon as he tried to listen closely to it.

"Can I get you anything?" Lilly asked.

"These lights are so bright. Maybe you could light that candle instead. And get me some more aspirin and a wet cloth for my head."

Lilly lit a candle and turned off the harsh overhead light. She brought him four aspirin. Funny, miracle painkillers came and went, but aspirin was still around, still the best.

Ben lay on the mattress and Lilly sat beside him, putting a cold compress on his forehead and rubbing his neck. His headache subsided a little and he perhaps he dozed. It was a strange state of half-consciousness, half-dream, warm and pleasant as the pain receded.

He dreamed he was flying his plane over San Francisco Bay, heading north toward Santa Rosa, over the old marshlands, now Novato Bay and Possum Straits. The golden gate was to his left, but it was the old orange one from before the quake, not the new silver one. Stinson beach and Bolinas Lagoon were still there, no Tomales Pass. As he flew, he saw the orange bridge crumple and the Pacific and Tomales bay roll over the tidelands and fill them in. The Petaluma River split like the skin of an overripe tomato and water rushed north over Novato to Cotati. Ahead of him the tall buildings of Santa Rosa waved like wheat in the wind, and a fine haze of dust rose up from the land. He flew straight downtown to the Kalimer building, going into a power descent and aiming for the eighteenth floor and Trujib Kapoor's office. As he got closer and closer, he could see Trudge and Sylvester Jones and Cynthia Lim in the eighteenth floor window. He crashed through the glass and the dream erupted in white light and evaporated.

Lilly was still beside him, reading Huckleberry Finn by candlelight. She looked like a pre-Raphaelite angel with her hair falling forward, her delicate hand reaching out to slowly turn a page, the graceful way she tipped her head from side to side, her lips moving slightly as she sounded out the harder words.

Ben realized that he had an enormous erection, that he was dying to reach up and take her in his arms, pull her down to him and rut like an animal.

He was horrified.

Lilly noticed that he was awake. She asked, "Are you feeling better?"

"Yes." Ben shifted so she wouldn't see his erection. "Headaches gone. I feel lots better."

"Let's read." She held out his link and the book. "Or I could read to you for a change. I'm getting lot's faster now."

If he linked with her, she'd know he was turned on to her. She'd feel repelled or at least confused. That would never do.

"I'm sorry Lilly. I don't really feel up to it right now. Maybe later."

"Okay." She went back to reading on her own.

Ben got up and hobbled over to the light switch, turned on the harsh overhead to kill the dangerous mood he was in.

"I'm going out for a walk," he said. "You all right here

179

for a while?"

"Sure."

Ben walked blindly through the blasted suburban landscape, stumbling over curbs, stepping in puddles, getting tangled in berry vines and old fencing. He might be a killer, but he was no pedophile, had never been attracted to little girls. His hormones must be really out of whack. This side effect was the last straw. If he kept taking Rejuven, he imagined how he might eventually rationalize making some kind of move on an eleven-year-old. It sickened him and at the same time held a dreadful attraction.

He had discovered the fountain of youth and dived right in. Nothing so far had prompted him to climb out, to shut off the fountain–not Glory's death, not following young women on the street, not fantasizing wild orgies and ridiculous scenes of triumph and justification, not even shooting Jones. He had been willing to be reckless and vainglorious, but he was not now ready to move on to perversion and abuse, to hurting someone he loved. Now he knew what would motivate him to shut off the fountain of youth. The "early adopter" would have to become an early abandoner.

He sat down on a retaining wall in front of a quake-damaged split-level rancher. Someone's prize rose bushes ran wild above him despite the choking weeds, and he could smell the sweetness of the blooms. His dream of perpetual youth was a mirage. He had to give up the delusion that he might somehow live forever young. He had to accept, again, that he, and everyone else, were going to die. Taking the long view, the whole species was going to die out eventually. It was all just a long experiment in adaptation and evolution, the currently viable solution to a problem with infinite solutions. He was one blip on a very large screen.

Thinking about death, Ben realized that his own death would be the perfect way to get back at Kalimer and scuttle Rejuven. He would see the headlines: "Side Effects Kill Drug Researcher." He wasn't depressed enough to commit suicide, but he was crazy and desperate enough to fake his own death. How could he "die" in a way that would really screw Kalimer?

52. Dynamite, at the Least

Ben went back to the apartment and went straight to his suitcase and took out his baggie of pills.

"What are you doing?" Lilly asked.

"Something I should have done a long time ago." He dumped the pills into the toilet and flushed it with the bucket. There were still so many that they almost clogged the old plumbing. He felt a pang of regret. It was like flushing his youth away, something he'd already done once in his life, and now had to do again.

"These were making me feel... too weird," he said. "It's time to straighten up and fly right. Or straighten up and fly wrong."

"That doesn't make any sense."

"I know, that's the beauty of it."

"You're still weird."

"Oh yeah?" Ben started rummaging in his bag, looking for Q-tips. "Here's a weird question for you then: Did you every imagine that you were dead, and everyone would miss you and feel sorry for you?"

"Like in Huckleberry Finn, when they're watching the people on the steamboat, looking for Huck's body?"

"Yeah, like that."

"Sometimes."

"Well, you and I are going to get to see what that's like. We're going to fake our own deaths, so that the cops will stop looking for us, and we'll start a whole new life, all over again."

"I don't understand."

"I'll explain as we go. First, I need a sample of your

DNA." He held up a Q-tip. "Open your mouth and say 'ahh-hhh.'"

He swabbed the inside of Lilly's cheek, collecting epithelial cells.

Lilly said something, but Ben couldn't understand it.

"What?"

"Are you going to clone me?"

"Not your whole body, just some cells."

"Cool. It's like Noam Ramen and The Drones."

"Say what?"

"This old band from the forties. They were dropping in the charts, so Ramen faked his death. They had a funeral and everything. Ramen was propped up in the coffin with his guitar. The rest of the band played their signature tune during the service, and Ramen sat up in the coffin and took his solo."

"Ours won't be quite so rock and roll."

"Drones were grunge roots, not R & R."

"Ours will be dynamite, at the least."

53. Fishing Wisdom

That evening Ben took his and Lilly's cell samples to the clinic where he had been working part time. It was after hours, but he still had his key. He snuck into the lab and started up two replicators. The machines would sequence their cheek lining cells and start pumping out undifferentiated stem cells. He routed the stem output into cloners that would make small but detectable amounts of muscle and bone tissue with their unique DNA signatures.

He left the equipment running and drove out to Louise's house in Santa Rosa. She was gone on a business trip overnight. He entered through the back door and did not turn on any lights. No one could know he was here. In the room that would have been their daughter's, if she had lived, he had a small workshop where he had built the avionics kits for their planes. By the light of small penlight he gathered up components and tools he would need. He put them into a gym bag and left in the dark, as silently as he had come.

If his plan was to work, Louise could never be told. It meant a complete and final break with her. That thought made his eyes water and his heart feel tight, constricted. He would never get over his guilt and regret about her, about all the chances they had past up, all the mistakes they had made, all the one-way, irreversible decisions between then and now.

He went back to the clinic at dawn and hid the accumulated tissues in the back of a refrigerator. He put everything back the way he found it. He would need two more nights to accumulate the material he needed. Meanwhile, he had work to do.

By day he stayed holed up in the apartment, sketching and calculating, soldering and crimping, occasionally looking something up online, but not ordering anything or otherwise leaving tracks. When he needed a component he didn't have, he sent Sylvia out to buy it for cash at one of the few surviving Radio Shacks, one in the Hayward Hills that served old-school computer geeks who had been flooded out of Silicon Valley and couldn't wait for the UPS truck. At night in the clinic, while the machines hummed in the background, he worked on his manifesto, the suicide note he would leave to screw Kalimer and throw the dogs off his trail.

As he toiled, he realized that he was happy. Scared and tired, yes, but happy too. He felt different, more like his old self. He was calmer and less distractible. This was what he was good at: seeing things through. Not leaving an experiment or a task unfinished, unresolved. Perseverance was a gift of age, standing in for the quick insight and blazing brilliance of youth when they were diminished or not immediately available.

The waning gifts of youth were like fish when you're fishing–sometimes biting, sometime not. The key thing was to keep fishing, put in the hours, keep your line in the water so you were ready when the fish of brilliance and insight got hungry. Over time, the best fishermen were not the youngest, the most clever, or the most knowledgeable. Over time, the best fishermen were the ones who went out fishing most frequently, spending more time with a line in the water.

54. Equals Boom

Ben thought that the explosives would be the hard part. Radio Shack didn't carry them and Sylvia warned him away from any internet research on the subject. Most surviving web sites offering up that sort of information were corporate trap sites, with flawed recipes and strong backtracker software to keep tabs on the dissatisfied.

"I asked around," Sylvia said. "Turns out explosives are cheap and easy here in the Maul. It's a commodity with low demand and high supply."

"Why is that?"

"The gear heads make a lot of biodiesel, and the pot heads have a lot of fertilizer for the phosphates."

"And you can make a bomb from that stuff?"

"I can't, but I know someone who can."

"You know some really interesting people."

"This might be a community of noncorporates–slackers, knackers, ne'er-do-wells, rakehells, dissidents, and divergents. But it is a community.

"Can we trust them?"

"We can trust the ones who are my friends."

"I don't have friends like that. I never have."

"I have five best friends. At least that's what they tell me."

"Amazing. My best friend is whomever I'm with. I don't have a long-term best friend. I tend to get close to whoever I'm working with on a project, then drift apart after the project is done."

"That's so typically male. Don't you ever hang out with the boys?"

"I'm no good at hanging out, being one of the boys. I don't like sports, don't like beer, don't like men, really, in some basic way. I've always had closer ties and better conversations with women."

"In my experience, that's typical of two types of guys: queers and intellectuals. They don't go for the macho stuff for some reason. They're too sensitive, or too smart."

"Or maybe they just lack the nads to run with the big dogs. I've always been the little dog on the lawn, watching the big dogs on the porch, wanting to join the pack."

""You're a big enough dog," she said, poking his arm. Then she poked it again. "You're stronger than you look, aren't you?" She squeezed his bicep.

"It's left over from the Rejuven. It won't last."

"Then you should use it while you've got it." She leaned into him.

He put his arm over Sylvia's shoulder, squatted a little, placed his other arm behind her knees, and lifted her easily off the ground, cradled in his arms.

"Wow." Sylvia looked into his eyes, then closed hers and tilted her head back, offering her lips.

They kissed. Ben carried her into the bedroom, enjoying the spring in his step despite the burden. Their lovemaking was deep and tender, less frantic than his fevered coupling with Louise, more like the best days and nights of Glory.

The next day six plastic milk jugs full of smelly gunk mysteriously appeared outside the door of Ben's squat, with a terse note wrapped around six little detonator sticks: "12 volts DC = BOOM."

Ben put the detonators under his mattress and stashed the jugs in the refrigerator, next to the plastic bags of tissue from the clone clinic. He was almost ready.

55. Remote Deployment

Ben parked the stolen car in front of his Mono Lake hangar. It seemed like years since he had been at the lake with Louise, but it had been fewer than six months. He opened the hangar doors to reveal his and Louise's tiny jets crouched side by side in the cramped space like birds in a box, eager to spring free and fly. They were coated with a thin film of dust, but otherwise everything was just as he had left it a lifetime ago.

He popped the canopy on his jet and hit the master switch. The solar trickle charger had kept the batteries up to voltage, so the instrument panel screens glowed to life. He plugged Glory's old handheld into the panel and synced it to the plane's computer. He thought Glory would appreciate this final sacrifice of her beloved 'vice.

He loaded the flight plan he had created. He superglued Glory's handheld to the windscreen with the camera looking forward and slightly down. To Glory's handheld he slaved an extra, untraceable handheld that Sylvia had provided. It displayed the view out the jet's windscreen, and duplicates of the primary flight screens.

Ben carried the handheld to the back of the hangar, plugged an old game controller, and moved the joystick up and down. The plane's stabilizer rose and descended smoothly. He moved the joystick left and right. The ailerons on the wing wig-wagged. Standing ten feet away, the response seemed instantaneous. At 300 miles, the lag time would be about one third of a second. Not good, but good enough. He tested several commands and made sure that the jet responded appropriately.

Ben didn't have a drone license, nor was his plane approved or equipped for remote flight. But the technology was pretty simple and had been around for decades, thanks to the military with their "interdictions" and "police actions" and "remote advisory deployments"—call them anything but "wars." The flight simulator and autopilot and wireless communication components were plentiful and robust, right off the shelf. Few pilots were reckless enough to try it because it voided your insurance, carried a million dollar fine, and lost you your pilot's license. Plus the lag time usually meant that you were likely to damage your plane during the most critical phase of any flight: the landing. Ben wasn't worried about the landing, the fines, his insurance, or his license. He had bigger fish to kill.

He carefully packed the plastic jugs of explosive into the nosecone, running wires back to the landing light switch, one of the functions he could control remotely. He dabbed his and Lilly's cloned DNA cultures all over the upholstery. Each of them was represented by about six ounces of pink hamburger. The authorities wouldn't recover any bodies, but DNA analysis would place both of them in the plane.

He pushed the plane out of the hangar and got in. He taxied out to the far end of the runway with the canopy open. Nobody was around, but if there were any concealed watchers, he wanted them to see him in the cockpit. He swung the plane around in the run-up area and set all the controls for takeoff.

He slipped out of the plane on the side furthest from the airport buildings and other hangars, slamming the canopy shut as quickly as he could. He crab-walked into the weeds at the side of the runway. Lying on his stomach, he was completely hidden in the knee-high growth. He worked the controls on Sylvia's 'vice. The engine went to full power and he released the brakes. The jet accelerated straight down the runway. At rotation speed Ben moved the virtual joystick back a little and the plane lifted smoothly into the air.

He climbed the plane to 12,000 feet and leveled off on a westerly course. From Mono Lake to Santa Rosa was a straight shot, 300 miles over the Sierras and across the Central Valley of California. Ben engaged the autopilot and shut off his handheld. He crawled through the weeds to the edge of the airport parking lot, stood up, and walked toward town.

Behind a warehouse in a deserted alley he powered up the handheld again and resumed control of the plane. The screen of the handheld was dim in the sunlit car, but he could make out key landmarks. It was like an old fashioned flight simulator.

He flew it to the Petaluma Estuary, then turned north up Novato Bay toward Santa Rosa. He homed in on the Kalimer building, its blue and green glass panels and anodized aluminum struts distinctive in the skyline along the bay. A half mile from shore, over the deepest part of the bay, he sent the signal to turn on the landing light. His screen turned to staticky mush as the camera and handheld and indeed the whole plane was reduced to flaming fragments and rained down into the water, well short of the shore and any buildings. He could see it in his mind almost as clearly as if he were in a rowboat on the bay.

Ben felt a wave of grief for his beloved homebuilt overwhelm him like a tsunami. Tears leaked out the outside corners of his eyes and he closed them. For several moments he sat in darkness and just listened to the wind blowing down the alley. Then turned off the handheld, walked slowly out to the main street and stuck out his thumb to hitchhike back to his new life.

56. Manifesto

"Sic Semper Tyrannis. Kalimer is Antichrist and Trujib Kapoor and Darius Jones are its apostles. I have slain the demon Jones in pure recompense for the murder of Gloria Banks. This is an act of justice for which I feel no guilt or compunction to atone. As for the destruction of Kalimer Tower, let it stand as a sign to all subjects of the Corporate Idol that the False God is Dead. As for my own demise, it is necessary and mete and just. My life was over when the first capsule of the poison "Rejuven" passed my lips. Let it serve as a sign to all Elders who come after me, not to reach for the gold ring of

Youth in the pill bottle. It is a Genie that must never be re-leased. If I can stop just one Soul from destroying yourselves with Rejuven, my death will not be in vain. It is a far far better thing I do than I have ever done before."

57. Flip Side

Ben, Lilly, and Sylvia were sprawled about in the Maul ex-Foot Locker, linked up three-way, catching up on the news, each in their own way. Ben was watching pirate satellite on a wall screen, since Glory's old handheld was in pieces at the bottom of the bay and Sylvia had made him ditch the burner handheld with all the flight apps on it. He didn't believe in all the urban legends about police net archives and covert digital fingerprints, but it made Sylvia happy to exercise her paranoia.

Lilly was wearing retro Headzup glasses, looking like a digital hippie from the thirties, courting a headache by beaming multichannel celebrity newsites straight to her retinas. Sylvia was mind-clicking from blog to blog, taking the pulse of the pulse-takers.

"It's pretty much unanimous," Sylvia said, "They all say you were crazy, on a bad Rejuven trip. Kalimer's firebreaks are completely overwhelmed. It's gone wildfire and they'll never contain it now."

"Here's one that says you read too many old books," Lilly said. "They blame Shakespeare and Disken."

"Dickens," Ben said, "Not Disken. We'll have to read David Copperfield."

"Who does he blog for?" Sylvia asked.

"Never mind."

Ben was quite proud of his fiery death and his Manifesto. The cheesy quotations, pseudo biblical language, and mixed metaphors caught the humorless grandiosity and manic mood of the artificial youth he had experienced while under the influence of Rejuven. There were lots of good "hooks" that broadcasters and bloggers had latched onto and run away with.

Police divers had raised fragments of the jet from the bay, he and Lilly's DNA were identified, and the murder case against him was closed. But all that was a sidebar to the flurry of sensational reporting and blogging about the drug-crazed suicide bomber pilot whose target was narrowly saved by his own incompetence.

"Kalimer stock just dipped under a hundred UN dollars," Sylvia said. "Even with Rejuven off the market, they're still in freefall."

"Any more purges?" Ben asked.

"Two more R&D types were put on waivers."

"Hood and Duchene?" Lilly asked.

"Yeah, that's them."

"That's fake. They just signed with InMates and they're going to be in a special two-hour episode next week."

Ben was disappointed about the reality TV show. It's ratings were climbing as fast as Kalimer stock was dropping. No silver lining was without a cloud. At least Trujib Kapoor and Cynthia Lim had been purged. Kapoor was demoted and transferred to the poultry antibiotic unit in Boise Idaho. Cynthia Lim was put on waivers and picked up by an online university with delusions of research.

Ben asked Sylvia to check his ex-wife Louise's credit score.

"It's up to 650," she said. "and her mortgages are shown as paid now."

"Good for her. She must have threatened to sue Kalimer for driving her husband crazy."

"Right, and they settled out of court by abrogating the mortgages. I hate to admit it, but she's a smart lady." Sylvia closed the page. "And that's the last time I'm checking. Best to keep our fingerprints off her."

"All right." Ben said. "It looks like she came out okay."

Ben felt guilty for all the pain he had caused Louise, up to and including "dying" suddenly. But she was better off now. She could bury herself in her watershed work and hopefully to never hear the name of Kalimer or Ben Rasmussen again.

"What do you think of the name Brad Studmuffin?" Ben asked Sylvia.

She threw a pillow at him. "Besides sounding too much like Ben Rasmussen, it's completely implausible. How about Limp Dickfield?"

"Puleeze!" Lilly said. "You two are so gross. I'm picking the new names, and that's final. I'm going to be Anastasia Finn, and I'm going to be twenty-one years old." Sylvia threw another pillow at her.

Ben sat back and laughed. He realized that he felt happy and relaxed for the first time in months, just hanging out with his new family.

"What about you, Ben?" Sylvia asked, "What age do you want to be?"

"My real age. Sixty. Sixty-one next Wednesday. Not a day older, but not a day younger either."

Patrick Fanning

Epilogue

Patrick Fanning

58. Leaky Faucet of Youth

Ben's name was Jack now, Jack Benson. Good old Doctor Jack, the guy at Ray's Community Health Clinic. Three days a week he practiced as a doctor in all but name, scanning patients, running tests, and mostly talking to people, especially older people. He didn't call them patients or clients or covered lives. He didn't call them anything out loud, but in his mind they were part of his extended family.

One of his favorites was Marjorie, a seventy-five-year-old woman who had been a dancer in her younger days. She came in for a followup visit and he automatically handed her a clinic link set to put on.

"Oh Goody," Marjorie said, "Instant bedside manner."

"That may be," Ben said, "but I'll use anything that works."

"So you think people who link all the time are really healthier? Not just emo junkies?" She settled the link over her ears.

"I've watched a couple of studies on the net. Seems to be true that linkers are a little better off, mentally and physically." Ben turned his handheld so that they both could see the screen.

"Look right here," he said, enlarging and rotating part of the image of Marjorie's spine. "this vertebra is starting to collapse, from the osteoporosis."

She leaned forward and peered at the screen, looking over the top of her glasses, her nose almost touching Ben's handheld.

"Oh dear. That looks bad."

Ben patted her hand and turned off the handheld.

"It's not so bad," he said. "Just keep taking the calcium and doing your exercises. You're doing a good job of keeping the muscles around your spine strong enough to hold everything together. And you can try these." He gave her an unmarked bottle of pills.

"What are they?"

"A little cocktail I take myself. It'll make your cartilage a little thicker, elevate your mood a bit, and damp down inflammation. That's all. It won't touch your genes or refold any proteins. You're better off without that, believe me."

"How much are these? I'm on a tight budget, you know."

"It's my gift to you. If you like them, stop by next month and I'll give you more."

"Thank you."

"Don't get too excited. These aren't the Fountain of Youth. They're more like the Leaky Faucet of Youth. You'll get a few drops of relief, feel a little better."

"Remember that Rejuver drug? A few years ago? For a while it seemed like you could live forever."

"It was a dream. Nobody lives forever. If we were immortal, we wouldn't be human."

"Some redwoods live two thousand years."

"But not forever." Ben took off his link and closed the scan.

"How long would you live, if you could?" Marjorie asked.

"I don't know. Not forever. Longevity is a good thing,

but immortality is too long."

"Two thousand years?"

"No, I'm not as phlegmatic as a redwood."

"Two hundred?" She put the pills in the her purse and took off her link.

"That would be okay. If a turtle can handle two centuries, maybe I could too." He showed her to the door.

"Thanks, Jack. You're a tonic."

59. Brainz

Ben woke up and went to pee for the second time that night. His nights were interrupted once or twice by needing to get up and pee, as his prostate resumed its familiar irritation of his urethra. But he didn't mind. Except for the brief pee breaks, he slept well. He felt safe in their current hideout, an old storefront in a derelict strip mall. He and Sylvia were sleeping on a salvaged mattress behind the sales counter, and he could hear Lilly breathing softly on her air mattress in the back room. He felt comfortably old and paternal or avuncular or whatever toward Lilly, no longer weirdly attracted.

He wasn't sleepy, so he fired up his 'vice and checked out the latest episode of InMates-L. Li'l Piece tossed her blonde ringlets out of her face in her signature gesture, cracked her bubblegum, and slipped her arm around a new girl covered in smart tattoos and wearing an off-the-rack orange jumpsuit.

"Since y'all are quintessentially fresh meat here," Li'l Piece said, "allow me the effrontery to orient your ass."

"You sayin' what?" the new girl asked.

"I'm saying' you naïve, you way susceptible to getting in trouble."

"Suscepti-what?"

"Honey, you gotta work on your vocabulary. You gotta

get youself in the Brainz study, smarten you up."

There was no more mention of Rejuven. Its rocket-like rise in interest and popularity and been followed very quickly by a meteoric plunge into obscurity. Now the drug trial subplot was all about Brainz, a Service Pharm concoction intended to raise IQ.

Ben wondered about the side effects. They'd probably show up next season.

60. More Like a Tree

"I've got a line on a new squat for us," Sylvia said. "It's a real house, in the country, with a garden and everything."

"What's the downside?" Ben asked. There was always a downside. That's why they were squats. He and Sylvia and Lilly had been upwardly mobile for some time now, moving from the windowless garage to a condemned-by-the-health-depart-ment delicatessen, to a bankrupt teddy bear factory store, to the double wide mobile home the were currently in, with one room sealed off with tape and plastic sheeting to keep out the black mold.

"No downside for us" Sylvia said, "It's a regular house in Woodside, used to be the guest house on a big estate, so it's hidden from the road, way back in the woods. It fell off the rolls years ago after a fire. But since then it's been fixed up, bit by bit."

"You said no downside for us. Who's got the down-side?"

"The owner. She can't report the rental income, or even admit the house exists, so she keeps it in the squat communi-ty."

"She's not some most-wanted fugitive, doing DIY plas-tic surgery and hiding from the execution drones?"

"Nah, she's just this old disability scammer who can't report the rent."

"We'll actually be paying rent, like real citizens?"

"Yeah." Sylvia sounded defensive. "What's wrong with that? We can afford it now."

"Not a thing wrong with it." Ben grinned and gave her a big hug. "As long as it won't compromise our outlaw status. It just doesn't sound like a squat. Sounds more like a home."

"Now you're teasing me," she said.

"I know, isn't it fun?" he stood alongside her, arm around her waist, gently bumping hips. She was a good fit.

"Seriously, this is a great place, and you're going to love it. The rent isn't that much, because the owner also wants us to keep an eye on the property, and help her clear out her old barn."

"Sounds great. Let's take it."

They moved in the next weekend. Every time they moved, it took longer. They were accumulating stuff at a rapid rate. Lilly now had a bicycle, a giant stuffed panda, and a vintage game console that she could not bear to leave behind. Sylvia had a guitar and a mandolin she'd picked up somewhere along the way, and a fancy chox maker Ben had found, repaired, and given her as a surprise gift on her birthday. Ben had two tote bags full of tools, and he was thinking of looking for a steel toolbox to keep them in. Life on the run was slowing down to a walk.

"Can't you see it?" Sylvia said, packing up the chox maker. "We're becoming all greedy and acquisitive, just like... consumers."

"Just like a family," Ben said, slipping his arms around her from behind and kissing her neck. "Want to leave that chox thingy behind?"

"Just shut up. All I'm saying is, we're supposed to be keeping a low profile, living light, a small footprint, staying underground, remember?"

"I know that was the plan. But we're not corpses. We're

seeds. We're just sprouting and growing."

"Very poetic. Maybe you should start packing your tools."

Ben hefted the two satchels of tools and felt a twinge in his back. He decided to carry one at a time. Time was taking away the extra muscle mass that Rejuven had given him and he had to be careful.

He thought about what he had said to Sylvia, about them all being seeds. He realized that his mental image of the three of them was not topographical at all. A static image didn't capture it. Their life together was alive, moving and growing and changing. More like a tree, the roots burrowing deeper and deeper into the earth and drawing in the water of life, the trunk and branches and leaves reaching for the sun.

61. Piece by Piece

Their new landlord was Betsy, a gray-haired, elfin woman of seventy. She handed Ben a shovel and Lilly a hoe so they could clear weeds and dirt away from the barn door.

"I usually just squeeze through," she said, "but you'll need it all the way open to clean this mess out."

When they had cleared most of the weeds, Ben lifted up on the old wooden double doors and dragged them open. Rocks and roots snagged the bottoms of the doors and they had to do some more chopping and shoveling, raising a cloud of dust. Finally the doors were open. Sunlight slanted into the barn to reveal old lawnmowers, sagging shelving units, piles of lumber, stacked cardboard boxes, stacks of mismatched chairs—all covered with a layer of dun dust and wispy gray cobwebs. Lilly found a light switch and turned it on. A few old fluorescent shop light fixtures started humming and fizzing, and about one tube in three came on.

"All this junk has to go," Betsy said. "Recycling, flea market, the dump, I don't care."

"Some of this stuff is still good," Ben said.

"I know, but I don't have any use for it. It was my husband's stuff. He's been dead ten years now, and I haven't even gone into the barn for a couple of years."

"I can use some of these tools, and we could sell some stuff at the flea market."   "Anything you can use, it's yours. Anything you sell, I'll split the money with you fifty-fifty. I just don't want to have to go through it myself." She left, stumping off toward her car. She lived in town with her daughter.

Ben and Lilly waded into the mess, dragging furniture and lumber and boxes out into the light and sorting them into big piles to go to the dump, to be cleaned and fixed and used, to sell online, to take to the flea market. At the back of barn, parked in a horse stall, was an old gas car under a dusty cover. Ben pulled back the cloth and saw the familiar scooped headlight of a Datsun 240Z.

"Lilly, come here and look at this," he said, whipping the cover off in a giant cloud of dust.

"What's that old thing?" Lilly asked. She sneezed.

"Glossiest car ever. Datsun 240Z, from 1969 or thereabouts. My dad had one like it."

"Will it run?"

"Probably not. It looks a little rough. See here, the paint is scorched by a fire or something. And this window is cracked." He opened the driver's door and popped the hood. "Engine looks complete, and the interior's all there. I'll bet we could fix this up and get it running like new again."

"Glossy. I like the color, orange is so happy."

"Wait, there's another one back here." In the next stall over, under a layer of flattened cardboard boxes, was another Datsun. "This is the parts car," Ben said after shoving the cardboard to the floor. It's a later model, a 280Z from the seventies. Not as desirable, but a lot of the same parts."

Weeks later, when the barn was more or less cleaned out,

they pushed the orange Z car out of its stall and into the middle of the space, where Lilly had swept the concrete floor and consolidated the working light tubes to provide better illumination. Ben dragged over an old kitchen table and set his new steel toolbox on top. He handed Lilly a pad of yellow lined paper, a roll of paper tape, a box of manila envelopes, and a grease pencil.

"You're going to take notes as we dismantle the car," he said, "Write down each part as we remove it and put it in a bag or put a tape label on the big parts. Label the bags with the pencil. We'll figure out a code to indicate which parts we'll clean and put back on, which will have to be replaced, and which need rebuilding."

"How will we know which is which?"

"We'll learn as we go. This will help." He handed her a stack of papers he'd printed out. "This is a copy of the original Service Manual."

She looked at the paper and bags. "It's kind of old fashioned, isn't it? Can't I just put it all in my handheld?"

"No, you'll get your handheld all greasy. Paper is better for this kind of job. Anyway, this car comes from before computers. Not a silicon chip in it anywhere. It's more respectful to keep paper records." Ben had an ulterior motive. By making Lilly read the paper manual and take notes and keep records, it would improve her reading and writing. She could not fall back on the iconics of her handheld.

"Let's start in Section Three," he said, "Engine removal."

Lilly was slow at the start, puzzling over unfamiliar words and the peculiarities of a static, unsearchable manual made out of ink and dead trees. But her reading speed improved. Her handwriting in the yellow tablet and on the parts labels got smaller and neater. She reorganized the tablet into a five-column sequential log, with dates and addresses of when and where they sent the generator and starter to be rebuilt, the bumpers to be re-plated, and the cylinder head to be scanned and fitted with new valves.

"It's like a story," she said, "the history of the car."

"Or like time travel or running a movie backwards," Ben said. "At some point all these parts will start coming back, and we'll reinstall them in the reverse order."

"I should video it. We can do it like stop motion animation and make a movie of the car coming together."

"Good idea."

Sylvia showed Lilly how to put up an anonymous blog site featuring the restoration of her car. She put their photos online and corresponded with other people restoring similar cars. When they pulled the old engine block out, she made a video of the process, and likewise whenever they removed a major part. She was fastidious and methodical, insisting that they wear rubber gloves and clean all the grease off with orange oil solvent.

As the car went back together Lilly videoed and blogged about each step. She used all English text, no iconics, out of respect for the car she called "Betsy." They built up the L28 engine from the 1978 parts car, the largest, most powerful motor that would bolt into their 1969 frame. They scrapped the electronic fuel injection on the newer engine and used the old-school carburetors and distributor from the original engine.

"These round-top carbs really suck the gas," Ben said, "so we'll never be able to afford a long trip."

"I don't care," Lilly said. "As long as I can drive it to the beach when I'm sixteen." She already had her learner's permit, and Sylvia was teaching her to drive stick shift in Betsy's old jeep. They bounced around and around the old apple orchard, raising dust and laughing hysterically.

Ben was impressed by how Lilly had taken charge of the project. She reminded him of himself when he was young: focused, obsessive, driven.

"We have to take the whole dashboard out," Lilly said. They were staring through the windshield at the cracks in the plastic dashboard. "It's the only way to get at those cracks and fix them right."

"What does that involve?" Ben asked.

Lilly ran her finger down the manual on the hood. "You have to start by removing the glove box door and pulling out the cardboard liner. That gives you access to the wiring harness and you unplug it in several places. Then there's about sixteen screws and nuts to remove."

"You'll be working upside down under the dash." Ben said. "It's a nasty job, and I'm too old and stiff to do it anymore. It will be up to you."

"I can do it."

"I'm sure you could, But it's just going to crack again. Exposed all the time to the sun through the windshield, these dashes always crack. We could just throw a dash cover over the cracks. A black carpet cover is only like thirty dollars UN."

"No, I'd always know the cracks were there. It's like when Josh Ridley reformed Backlash. Their keyboardist left the band, and Josh could have just replaced him, but no. He disbanded the whole group, took it down to his guitar and the drummer, and spent a year putting their sound back together piece by piece. That's when MacReynolds and Bujo joined Backlash, and the next year they had their biggest hit, 'Regard-less.'"

"It's up to you," Ben said.

"I'll need the ten millimeter long socket," Lilly said, sliding into the passenger seat and opening the glove box door. "And that stubby Phillips screwdriver."

Ben stood outside the car, handing her tools. He was proud of her, her stubbornness and drive. It was like his own process with Rejuven, wanting to take people down to the frame and rebuilt them better than factory new. It was a big job, and they were just going to crack all over again. But he liked seeing Lilly make the effort. She was a genius that way.

62. A Spice, Not a Staple

"Remember," Sylvia said, putting her hand through the open driver's window and caressing Lilly's shoulder, "the cops are just looking for an excuse to bust an old gas car. Keep it under the limit."

Lilly grinned and gave her a thumbs up, racing the Z car's engine: Vroom vroom. Ben laughed from the passenger seat. "Don't worry," he told Sylvia, "I'll make sure she gets us back in once piece, no cops."

"You guys have a nice time," Sylvia said. "Happy birthday." She stepped back and Lilly wheeled the bright orange sports car sedately out of the barnyard and up the long curving gravel drive toward the road. She kept it slow and steady, not wanting to kick up any gravel and ding their freshly painted body work. Dust from the road plumed out behind them and drifted in the open windows.

"How does it feel?" Ben asked.

"Great."

"Driving the car, or being sixteen and legal?"

"Both." When they were on the paved road, Lilly gunned the car and worked smoothly up through the gears. Ben felt pushed back into his cushy vinyl seat at every gear change. The engine was throaty and loud in the old car, just like it was 1969 all over again. He cranked his window all the way down and leaned his seat back, letting the wind blow through his hair. It was all gray again, but he didn't care.

Lilly turned onto the deserted back road to the coast and opened it up a little more, down shifting and braking on the straights, accelerating through the curves, just like Ben and Sylvia had taught her.

"Whoo-eeeee," she yelled and Ben laughed with her.

He closed his eyes and felt the vibration of the road

through the stiff racing suspension, feeling every little pebble and seam in the old asphalt. He had to laugh at himself, thinking back over all the years he'd spent fighting aging, resisting death, not living. Neglecting the present to take care of an imaginary future. The future was always imaginary, had to be by its very nature. Imagination was a good thing, heady like spirits or drugs, but it was not sufficient in itself. You couldn't live on it. It was a spice, not a staple, he thought. The present moment, that's where all the nourishment is.

Then he stopped thinking. He settled back and just enjoyed the ride.

Rejuvenation